A Diabolic Promise...

"There are more than a dozen ways to kill a man in this room," Moriarty snarled. "Have you wondered why I have not employed any of these methods on you?"

"Well," Holmes offered dryly, "it's not for want of trying."

"No, Mr. Holmes—it's because it doesn't suit my book. I shall destroy you, but in *my* fashion! The crime of the century—the past century, this one, and all centuries to come—is now in preparation. It will go forward as planned, despite the temporary setback your interference has caused me. It will take place, Mr. Holmes, before your very eyes! AND YOU WILL BE POWERLESS TO PREVENT IT!"

SHERLOCK HOLMES IN NEW YORK is the ultimate battle of wits and wills in the annals of high crime... *and* high adventure!

SHERLOCK HOLMES IN NEW YORK

STARRING
Roger Moore as Sherlock Holmes
John Huston as Moriarty
Charlotte Rampling as Irene Adler
Patrick MacNee as Dr. Watson

Executive in Charge of Production Jack Haley, Jr.

Executive Producer Nancy Malone

Produced by John Cutts
Directed by Boris Sagal

SHERLOCK HOLMES
IN NEW YORK

By Alvin Sapinsley

Adapted by D. R. Benson

BALLANTINE BOOKS • NEW YORK

Copyright © 1976 by Twentieth Century-Fox Film Corporation

All rights reserved under International and Pan-American Copyright Conventions. Published in the United States by Ballantine Books, a division of Random House, Inc., New York, and simultaneously in Canada by Ballantine Books of Canada, Ltd., Toronto, Canada.

ISBN 0-345-25571-2-150

Manufactured in the United States of America

First Edition: October 1976

Foreword

Those readers who have been kind enough to divert themselves with my published accounts of the work of my friend Mr. Sherlock Holmes will naturally be surprised—I do not flatter myself so far as to say pleased—to find yet such another narrative offered to them at so late a date; a date at which, indeed, both Holmes and myself shall long have been one with the past.

I must say that, on this point at least, such a reader's vexation, if any, must be directed at the shade of Sherlock Holmes, not at that of his unassuming chronicler. He had, of course, in the past made many demands that the particulars of one case or another not be revealed until the passage of some years to protect the interests of those involved. Touching *this* adventure, he was at first adamant in insisting on an unprecedented fifty years' delay. "It touches not the foibles of rulers and statesmen, Watson," he observed, "but the very lifeblood of the intercourse of nations. Wars themselves do not so adversely affect world relationships as would any loss of confidence in the verities of international exchange. In fact, you had best make that seventy-five years' time; even fifty might not suffice to render the story innocuous." The alarming events of this year, culminating only days ago in the assassination of the American President, lend weight to the view that the peace and security of the world is to be a chancy matter in the twentieth century.

Therefore, though setting down the events which

follow but a few months after their occurrence, I will be obliged to respect Holmes' wishes so far as to make provision for my manuscript's strait concealment until the year 1976—a date which it is indeed startling to find myself committing to paper! Mr. H. G. Wells may deal comfortably with times so far in the future in his scientific romances, but I own an uneasiness in contemplating a date three-quarters and more through this new century. And yet—and here I believe I see a motive which Holmes will not admit, even to himself —one of the principals in the drama may yet still be living at that time, though past the stage in life where what is revealed could strongly affect him for good or ill. Should that be the case, I comply gladly with Holmes' wishes: it is not often granted to the friends of Mr. Sherlock Holmes to grant him a request arising from the normal emotions of humanity rather than from his acute and unsparing intellect.

One further word on my own role as Boswell to my friend's Johnson: I have always preferred to give a straightforward account of what I myself have seen and heard—medical men and detectives alike know the untrustworthiness of second-hand evidence!—but find that I am obliged to vary the rule in this case, in order to present certain significant events of which I became informed only much later, or, indeed, have been obliged to deduce from their effects. A certain conversation in a theatrical dressing-room, for instance, was never (and will never be, I am certain) revealed to me by Sherlock Holmes; yet it took place, and must have followed the course which will be described here. I, too, have my methods.

                    John H. Watson, M.D.
                    Baker Street, September, 1901

Chapter One

In the nearly sixty-four years of her reign, an uncounted number of places and objects of every size and kind were named for Alexandrina Victoria Wettin, Queen and Empress whose domain spanned the entire world: lakes, mountains, territories, monuments, the broad Embankment by the Thames, London's greatest railway station, even the smartest style of open carriage. Her name had, indeed, been given to a period in history, the Victorian Age.

That age was now a part of the past, and had been for nearly two months, since the old Queen's death toward the end of January. Emperors and kings, presidents and barbaric chieftains had flooded into London for the unprecedented pomp of the funeral, as much a celebration of the might of her Empire as a mark of respect for the woman who had ruled it. Whatever delights and wonders of the imperial capital the visitors savored, it may be safely assumed that few or none of them made their way to one of the more sinister, decayed, and dangerous locations to bear the Queen's name: Victoria Docks.

Choking yellow fog swirled above the cobbled alleys on this March night; the stones, where visible, glistened oilily as if coated with slime rather than water. With the bustle and clangor of daytime industry absent, the blank façades of docks and warehouses presented the impression of a city built in times long past and abandoned by its makers to crumble into mud and rubble.

Picking his way with care along the slick stones, a

man approached the most ruinous of the buildings facing the alley he traversed. It might have seemed as though he had lost his way thoroughly, for the fashionable evening dress, the richly lined cape that offered protection against the damp and chill, the burnished top hat, the ivory-handled cane—even the veined, bulbous nose and florid complexion which attested to a sybarite's indulgence in the pleasures of the table— would have been far better suited to the flaring lights of the Strand or Piccadilly or to the more discreet illumination of a private restaurant or Mayfair gaming house than to the feeble glimmer of the street lamps that shone only on decay and desolation.

Yet the man seemed sure of himself and his destination. As he neared the boarded-up warehouse, he glanced upward and nodded with satisfaction upon seeing a faint streak of yellow light at a second-floor window. He consulted his massive pocket watch and nodded again.

Abandoned and derelict the warehouse certainly appeared to be from its exterior. Yet the lamp whose light had attracted the notice of the approaching man was an elegantly wrought electric model elaborately ornamented with Egyptian motifs. It lit up brightly a room furnished with richly covered overstuffed chairs and divans, colorfully figured oriental carpets, and intricately carved decorations—a room which stated plainly in every detail that it was the dwelling of a man who valued, and could afford, luxury.

The householder himself did not appear to have extended his tastes to his own person: the brocade dressing gown gathered about his spare, stooped form was shabby and soiled, his seamed, vulpine face with its sharp nose and beady eyes was unthickened by rich food or drink, and the few wisps of pale gray hair clinging to his high-domed skull had not recently seen the attention of a barber. In his disorder, he resembled the popular idea of an impractical academician; and, indeed, Professor James Moriarty had won an international reputation for his contributions to mathematics, notably his treatise on *The Dynamics of an Asteroid*.

The richness of the room indicated a level of income higher than that of any scholar, however eminent, and the ornately framed blackboard on its wheeled stand in the center of the room bore calculations and figures which testified to the Professor's concerns with matters more practical than algebraic esoterica.

There were ten entries on the board:

1. Quint to Cavendish Square, 8.25.

2. Adelspate and Stryker to Eaton Place, 9.12.

3. Moran meet Bethune, 9.46, collect Nickers in 4-wheeler, Brompton Oratory, 10.2.

4. Ashby and Spinnerton follow LORD BRACKISH from Simpson's to Covent Garden, watch box and side entrance.

5. M., B., and N. meet A. and S., 10.36. A. transfer to hansom at Henrietta Street.

6. Moran in hansom, 4th in rank at C.G.

7. Ashby and Spinnerton steer LORD BRACKISH to Moran hansom at end of opera, between 11 and 11.15.

8. Hansom to Albert Memorial, LORD BRACKISH to be despatched by Moran during trip.

9. Quint, Adelspate, and Stryker to meet hansom at A.M., assist M. in disposal of body.

10. Moran to Moriarty with BRACKISH cigar case at midnight *exactly*.

The first eight entries bore neat check-marks before their indicating numbers.

Professor Moriarty consulted his watch, moved to the board, and, holding the chalk stick in practiced fingers, entered another check before the sentence that outlined his three underlings' role as clandestine undertakers: it was on the time-table, and the time had come and passed; he could therefore assume it had been accomplished. Few of those who served Professor Moriarty swerved from the schedule he established even once; none did so twice.

The Professor returned to his high-backed swivel chair behind the massive mahogany desk, picked up a balloon glass with an inch of brandy in it, swirled the amber-colored liquid, and savored the released aroma. This was the most enjoyable moment of all, to inhale the scent of anticipated triumph as he was now inhaling the fumes of the brandy. When the thing was done, it was well enough; but the last moments before consummation, knowing that the last perfecting touch was on the very point of falling into place— *that* was truly delicious!

As the hands of the tall clock in the corner joined in a single upward-pointing line and its machinery gave a soft whir and then began to chime, he rose, went to the door, and began to unfasten the bolts and locks that secured it. With the visitor he was expecting, there was no need to wait for a knock: when the time came, he would be there.

He flung the door open and, as he had known he would, saw a familiar, stocky figure before him, tall hat cocked at an arrogant angle, red-lined cape gathered about him, a glint of lamplight reflecting from the monocle screwed into the left eye.

"Colonel Moran! You are punctuality itself," Moriarty said, his words underlaid by the continuing strokes of the clock.

The man stepped inside the room and brushed one hand along the luxuriant gray moustache, waxed to spikes at the ends in the fashion favored by the late Queen's grandson, the Kaiser.

"Everything has proceeded according to schedule?" The Professor's tone was not really questioning.

The man reached into an inner pocket of his tail coat and drew out a cloisonné-work cigar case.

In a rasping voice that carried a history of orders

bawled out in drill or battle and of hard-drinking nights in regimental messes, he said cocking an eye at the blackboard, " 'Number ten. Moran to Moriarty with Brackish cigar case at midnight *exactly*.' "

He tapped a fingernail on the enamelled surface of the case.

The Professor gave a shrill, gobbling laugh, loped to the blackboard, and, with a force that crumbled a fragment from the end of the chalk, struck a broad line through the last sentence written there.

"Perfect!"

"With one exception, that is."

The voice that spoke was lower, firmer, and more even than the grating tone Moriarty had just heard; he whirled to face his visitor.

Colonel Sebastian Moran's distinctive nose now rested on the desk, like a misshapen, gigantic strawberry. As Moriarty watched, his eyebrows and moustache were detached, small, shaping pads of gutta-percha were removed from the cheeks, and the glittering monocle fell to dangle on the end of its cord.

The changeling stretched and allowed himself to assume his full height; from it, he looked down with sardonic amusement at the Professor, whose face was now distorted by rage and apprehension.

"A trifling exception, perhaps," he said gently. "I simply don't happen to be Colonel Moran."

The man stroked his hawk-like nose, removing a last trace of putty from it.

Moriarty's voice was hoarse and shaking. "Sherlock Holmes!"

The tall man looked at him almost benignly.

"At your service, Professor. I should be vexed that you did not recognize me, although it has been ten years since we met at the Reichenbach Falls. *Your* features, I assure you, have been graved on the tablets of my mind ever since, though I thought you dead in that plunge over the cliff. Well, well, I dare say that may be remedied in due course, with a shorter drop at the end of the hangman's rope!"

Holmes, now completely divested of his disguise, continued, "I can imagine the profundity of your disappointment. You cannot possibly fail to realize that there can be only one explanation for my having successfully penetrated the most carefully concealed lodgings in the whole of London." He looked around the elaborately furnished room with an expression of distaste. "I observe that your choice of decoration is fully as disagreeable as your choice of profession."

Professor Moriarty was past taking exception to criticism of his taste by a man who adorned his own walls with designs in bullet-pocks and kept his tobacco in an old Persian slipper. He was nearly hissing with rage as he moved closer to Holmes.

"Where is Colonel Moran!"

"He is in custody." Holmes strode to the blackboard, and, with a mocking imitation of a pedagogue correcting a pupil's botched work, slashed heavy lines through each chalked item thereon. "As are Quint, Adelspate, Nickers, and Stryker!" He turned to Moriarty. "In short, your entire organization here in London is now occupying cells at the Bow Street Police Station—*and* the assassination of Lord Brackish has failed!"

He whirled to face the blackboard once more, snatched up the erasing cloth that lay on the stand, and swept it across the chalked surface twice diagonally, leaving an X slashed through the Professor's meticulous time-table.

"Damn and blast you for the meddler you are, sir!" Moriarty sawed the air impotently with white-knuckled fists, and his voice, rising to a near scream, drew unconsciously on the mode of speech of a long-forgotten past. "With your West End ways, talkin' down your upper-class nose, and only happy when you're dressin' up as someone else—as though life was some schoolboy lark! Blast you, Holmes! Blast you!"

"I suggest you make an effort to take hold of yourself," said Sherlock Holmes. "Your rage is beginning to affect your speech."

Moriarty drew a deep breath and, with a visible effort, stilled the trembling that agitated his form. His eyes narrowed, and stayed fixed on Holmes as he himself moved sideways, in gait unpleasantly resembling a crab, to the chair behind his desk. Picking up a neelde-sharp brass letter-opener, he toyed with it. When he spoke, his voice was once more controlled, even, and cultured.

"Did you come alone tonight?"

"Since you ask, yes."

"I thought as much. I know your methods by now. Your inability to resist the *tour de force,* the *coup de grâce,* the necessity of nourishing your egotism unassisted."

Holmes, seemingly indifferent to this diagnosis of his character, had picked up from the mantel a vase decorated in the Chinese manner, with acid green and ox-blood dominating the color scheme.

"Atrocious," he murmured, inspecting it closely. He looked from it to its owner, and added, "As is your French. I fancy the term you were reaching for is *coup de main.* What I truly regret is that I must also *leave* alone. Your cohorts refuse to implicate you, and Moran, indeed, fears for his life—justly so, I imagine —should he do so. And, troublesome though it is, I thank God that British justice requires the strongest evidence to bring to book even such scoundrels as yourself."

His face stern, he pointed the vase toward Moriarty as though it were a cannon.

"But be warned, Professor! Your people have been captured, and you are alone! Alone and helpless, and I will have you yet!"

Holmes emphatically set the vase down on a table; it shattered into a pile of gaudy shards. He looked at it as though feeling its present state was better than its last.

Moriarty's hooded eyes glared at him with unwinking malice.

"Mr. Holmes, your interference in my affairs has gradually grown from mild annoyance to insufferable impertinence. And tonight's actions have finally rendered you intolerable to me!"

"Really?" Holmes' voice was a calculated drawl of languid surprise. "Only tonight? You, sir, have been intolerable to me for *much* longer than that."

Moriarty's hand shifted in a sudden tugging motion behind the desk.

"Mr. Holmes, if you'll be good enough to observe —this!"

A square section of flooring next to the wall, four feet on each side, dropped away. From below, a swirl of water around decaying pilings could be heard, and a gust of the dank odor of the Thames entered the room. Sherlock Holmes looked at the open trap door with polite interest.

"And this!"

Professor Moriarty stabbed at a push-button on the desk. There came a whir and a *thock!* A heavy dart with half its four-inch point buried in the wall by the force of its flight quivered less than an inch from Holmes' head. He inspected it with raised eyebrows.

"This!"

The Professor pulled a lever set into the side of the desk, and the crystal-festooned chandelier that hung from the center of the ceiling crashed to the floor, scattering glittering shrapnel across the room. Holmes leaned down and flicked a splinter of glass from his trousers.

"Not to mention—this!"

Moriarty's hand darted into a desk drawer with the speed of a striking snake, and emerged holding a revolver, which he levelled at the detective.

"There are more than a dozen ways to kill a man in this room," he went on, "and the trap door into the Thames will remove all traces of the man's ever having been here. Have you wondered why I have not employed any of these methods on you?"

"Well, it's not for want of trying," observed Sherlock Holmes, surveying the opening in the floor, the heavy dart embedded in the wall, the ruin of glass and wiring on the floor, and the pistol in the Professor's hand.

"No, Mr. Holmes—it's because it doesn't suit my book. I *shall* destroy you, but in *my* fashion!"

"Will you, indeed?" said Holmes, much as a man might express interest in a neighbor's plans to cultivate a prize-winning vegetable marrow.

"Yes! I am going to crush you in such a way that your humiliation and downfall will be witnessed by the entire world!"

"How fascinating! And just how do you propose to do that?"

"The crime of the century—the past century, this one, and all centuries yet to come!—is now in preparation. It will go forward as planned, despite the temporary setback your interference tonight has caused me. It will go forward, it will take place, and, Mr. Holmes . . . *it will take place before your very eyes!* And you will be powerless to prevent it!"

He sat back in his chair, gesturing with the revolver as though driving home a salient point of mathematics in the classroom.

"The world will gape at its very immensity! And when the world discovers that it has occurred within arm's length of the incomparable Sherlock Holmes, the world will *sneer,* the world will ridicule—and the world will hound you into oblivion! *That* is why I have not used any of the means at my disposal here in this room. *I have other plans for you, Mr. Sherlock Holmes!"*

The Professor sank back further, in his chair, fairly panting with the emotion that had surged through him in the course of his tirade. Holmes looked at him for a moment, then slowly shook his head.

"Have you? I, on the other hand, have the same

plan for you that I have always had: to see you swing at the end of the hangman's rope. I have no doubt, Professor, that it is *my* plan that will prevail."

He stood above the wizened Professor for a moment, a brooding sternness shadowing his face. He might have been an avenging angel taking the measure of a demon of the Pit for a fated forthcoming struggle.

A piece of crystal crunched under one evening pump as he shifted his stance slightly. He glanced down, and his face lightened with a wry smile.

"Pity about the chandelier. It was the only thing in the room that showed a *little* style. Don't bother to get up, Professor. I'll see myself out."

He turned and was gone from the room.

Professor Moriarty sat for many minutes, his clawlike hands cradling the blued metal of the revolver with an almost urgent affection, gazing with a curiously passionless abstraction at a point in space between himself and the wall. Then, moving decisively, he laid down the weapon and strode to the blackboard. Wiping it clean, he picked up the chalk and began charting his next project in large but meticulously neat letters:

1. SHERLOCK HOLMES TO ...

Chapter Two

Some three days after the singular confrontation just described, on the 22nd of March of this year of 1901 to be precise, a dismal morning found me finishing a quite satisfactory breakfast in the lodgings I had so often shared with Sherlock Holmes. The practice of my profession, and two marriages which left me twice a widower, had seen me domiciled elsewhere for long periods of time, but I was well aware that the cluttered rooms at 221B Baker Street were now truly my home, and one which suited me eminently. Mrs. Hudson is a jewel of a landlady, with a rare understanding of the sort of breakfast required to start a day; and, trying though he is at times, Sherlock Holmes is a fellow-tenant of the kind guaranteed to keep a constitutionally torpid medical man stimulated and on his toes!

As he entered the sitting room, where breakfast had been laid, however, he seemed sunk in morose introspection, and flung me a glum " 'Morning, Watson. Breakfasting?" His faded purple dressing-gown hung on him a little. "Now how, Holmes," said I gravely, "did you work that out?"

I took a sip of my tea and returned to my perusal of *The Times,* anticipating a small surprise its pages had in store for him.

Sherlock Holmes was in no mood for persiflage.

"Watson, do you mind curbing your tendency toward schoolboy jokes for the moment? You know I've no head for humor when there's nothing to occupy me but staring at rain-streaked windows on the other side of the street! Three days since I broke the back of

Moriarty's organization, and there's not been a caller or a letter worthy of my attention!"

Hands behind his back, his head bowed, he strode across the room to the bookshelf and cast a sour glance at the bound volumes containing those cases of his which, with a constantly expressed distaste and reluctance (though, I have always felt, a secret pride) he allowed me to present to the public gaze.

He ran his finger along the gilded tops of the books as if looking, indeed hoping, to discover dust, and observed, "As my biographer, Watson, you've precious little with which to occupy yourself these days. You'll soon be afflicted with the same boredom I'm suffering, I dare say, though I don't suppose you're quite as congenial a host to the blue devils as I am. I tell you, it's intolerable! If nothing is to happen for the moment in the matter of Professor Moriarty, so be it. For the big game, after all, one must be prepared to wait in the blind for as long as needs be.

"Yet has London lost its flavor with the Queen's passing? Where are the ingenious stranglers, the convoluted cracksmen, the bizarre blackmailers of yesteryear? Why, the new King's cronies by themselves ought to account for a torrent of activity ready-made for a consulting detective!"

Though I was as aware as he that, as Prince of Wales, the King had acquired many dubious associates, I was not well pleased with Holmes' comment. I had, as Holmes had not, worn the uniform of my country, and preferred to consider my monarch as beyond the reach of a subject's light censure; though I admit that His Majesty Edward VII may well test this principle farther than I would like, before his reign is done.

I let my friend's remark go by, and said merely, "Well, well, I'm certain matters will look up before long." I allowed a note of smugness to creep into my voice as I added, "And, by the bye, within a fortnight's time you will be receiving a letter from America."

Holmes turned from the bookcase and bent on me a glance which mingled impatience, surprise, and a trace of hope that something of interest might after all be in the wind.

"How in the world do you come to know such a thing?"

"Stealing a bit of your thunder, am I, Holmes? Mystified you, have I?" said I.

"Thoroughly."

I picked up the newspaper and said, "Well, then, listen to this item in the theatrical news: 'Our Broadway correspondent reports that on the thirty-first of this month Daniel Furman's production of Sir Arthur Wing Pinero's *The Second Mrs. Tanqueray* will open at the Empire Theater in New York.' Why do you suppose, Holmes, that the Americans would name a theater 'Empire' when they're a republic? No matter," for I saw a glint in his eye and a tightening of his mouth that bespoke a brusque response to this, to my mind quite legitimate, inquiry. "Ah, yes. 'In addition to Mr. Kendal, Mr. Huntley, Mr. East, and Miss Campbell, the distinguished cast will include, in her first non-singing role—' "

"Miss Irene Adler!"

I was dashed, and said so as I laid down the paper. "Holmes, I was dead set on astonishing you!"

"You have, Watson, you have," said Sherlock Holmes, his face animated in a way that, in spite of my disappointment that his nimble mind had divined my surprise, gladdened me. "Your ability to extract the single item of unalloyed interest from the entire mass of wordage in today's number of *The Times* is an astonishing faculty." He turned and strode briskly toward the mantelpiece.

I sighed as I laid down the paper and reflected on my friend's narrow scope of concern. "The one item of unalloyed interest," indeed! Aside from the progress of the war in South Africa, the contentions of Turk, Greek, and Bulgar in the Balkans, and a pungent if erratic speech by young Mr. Churchill in Commons, there was a most fascinating analysis by the financial correspondent of the prospects of the largest steel company in the world, just formed by Mr. Pierpont Morgan in New York, to be called United States Steel. Though not as sound as Consols, naturally, it seemed to me as though a share or so would not be an imprudent investment. But such matters are always far from the mind of Sherlock Holmes!

Standing at the mantel, he lifted up from it a dainty music-box ornamented in porcelain and gold filigree of such delicacy that it might have been spun sugar. It was emblematic of that cloying fusion of Germanic and Mediterranean taste that characterizes Franz Josef's empire. (As I write, it strikes me that the seemingly eternal Franz Josef, Wilhelm of Germany, Nicholas of the Russias, the Empress of China, the Sultan of Turkey, the Kings of Spain, Portugal, and Italy—every ruler now living—will be gone by the time this account is published. Who will sit on those thrones in that distant time, I wonder?) Holmes opened the box, and, faint and tinny, the strains of "Drink to Me Only with Thine Eyes" wafted through the room. It is a sentimental tune, but English to the core, and I have always thought it was that which prompted Irene Adler to make a present of this particular music-box to Holmes. European of the Europeans, she was; and Holmes, for all his half-French ancestry and occasional impatience with his more stolid countrymen, including myself, is as British as roast beef, impossible to imagine as a German, an Italian, or an American. I believe Irene Adler recognized this and chose to make him a gift that showed she did so.

Why, of course (being probably the only person, and assuredly the only woman, who had ever bested Holmes in the course of his work), she had felt it necessary to bestow this memento of their encounter on him was a more difficult matter to fathom. She had won the game fairly, and, in so doing, showed herself to have a stronger character and higher standards of conduct, admitted adventuress though she was, than the titled personage on whose behalf Holmes had been induced to act against her. In the baker's dozen of years that had passed since that "Scandal in Bohemia," Holmes had always referred to her as *"the* woman." Her opinion of him had been suggested by the gift of the music-box, and by certain envelopes received at irregular intervals.

Such an envelope—one of ten or so—Sherlock Holmes now removed from the filigreed box, and opened. I knew that, no matter which envelope it was, it contained two tickets from any one of a number of theaters in cities around the Continent and England, for dates ranging back nearly ten years.

"She's never failed to send you opening-night tickets, has she?" said I.

"Never," answered Holmes in a low voice. "Row E, seats one and three—for the last nine seasons." He replaced the tickets in their envelope and the envelope in its box, and continued in a musing, almost wistful tone, "One day we must find ourselves in those seats, eh, Watson? They've gone begging too long, far too long— Come in!"

Mrs. Hudson, after her discreet knock at our sitting-room door and Holmes' response, entered, clutching a large handful of envelopes.

"The post's come, sir," said she, and handed them to him.

As always, I could not repress a twinge of annoyance. Holmes and I shared the expenses of the household on a completely equal basis, and it was indeed I who saw to it that Mrs. Hudson's charges were met to the penny and to the date. Yet she made no secret of the fact that she regarded Holmes as the sole tenant of her rooms and myself as a welcome but inconsequential appendage. I knew that Holmes would, of course, pass over any letters or circulars addressed to me, but that was not the point: I should have much preferred Mrs. Hudson to separate our post and hand each man's to him directly. It was all the more galling that

I could not bring the matter up without appearing petty.

"Shall I bring some hot tea?" said Mrs. Hudson.

My cup was then quite cold, and the little tea remaining in the pot was scarcely more than a tepid stew of leaves.

"Why, yes, that would—"

"Yes, thank you, Mrs. Hudson," Holmes interrupted, leafing through the envelopes, "and if you've got a couple of rashers of streaky bacon, I'll—"

He stopped and held up an envelope bearing a stamp which I could see at a glance was not British.

"You must apologize to the trans-Atlantic mails, Watson. Your estimate of a fortnight for a letter from America lacks thirteen days of proving accurate."

I could sense his excitement as he slit the envelope, drew from within it a smaller one, and opened that.

"Row E as usual," said I. "Seats one and— Holmes, what is it?"

For I had seen the animated hands suddenly stop their motion, and a wary, shadowed look appear on the keen face, a look that deepened into dread as he inverted the smaller envelope over his open hand and shook from it a number of torn strips of pasteboard.

I rose and inspected the fragments. They were obviously the remnants of theater tickets and I could make out a clearly identifiable portion of a capital letter E.

"Good heavens, Holmes!" I exclaimed. "That's a rum business! Whatever would make her do a thing like that?"

My words seemed to galvanize Sherlock Holmes from his inactivity.

"Watson! There's not a moment to be lost. I must set out for New York this very day. Will you be kind enough to engage passage immediately?"

"Certainly, Holmes," I replied. "If time is of the essence, we can gain half a day by taking a Cunarder from Liverpool. The trains there are—"

"We? I said nothing of—"

"You cannot imagine," said I firmly, "that I shall allow you to embark on a matter of this moment—though what it is, I confess I do not know—unaccompanied. Especially in a strange country, you will need someone—"

"—on whom I can rely absolutely. You have the right of it, Watson, as always when it comes to questions not requiring over-much mental agility! Well, well, I shan't deny I shall be glad to have you by my side, though I warn you this is a dark business. I can't see the shape of it yet, but it may well be that we come away from it with worse wounds than that Jezail bullet-hole in your leg!"

It was not only Holmes' comment that reminded me of my Army service that morning; I own that I felt quite like a commanding officer planning an attack as I studied time-tables and sailing schedules, bullied the steamship line's clerk into telegraphing Liverpool to confirm our cabin, and arranged matters so that we would be on the high seas on a fast liner before sunset—with the great port of New York only six days and some hours ahead of us. I had even ferreted out from the clerk the means by which we were to get to the American city itself from our landing place on the opposite bank of the river, which bore the exotic name of Hoboken—there were frequent ferries, he assured me. I arranged for him to book rooms for us at an hotel by trans-Atlantic cable.

The sums of money I was obliged to lay out gave me pause, but did not deter me. This was clearly a matter of such urgency for Holmes that speed and speed alone was important. I counted myself lucky to live in an age when money *could* transport one across the ocean in practically the twinkling of an eye —less than a week.

It all went perfectly, with our trunks being tossed aboard the luggage van a full five minutes before our Liverpool train left Waterloo Station. As we stood on the platform before entering our carriage, a slight figure swathed in an ulster sprinted toward us.

"Mr. Holmes!"

"Why, it's Lestrade! Good morning, Inspector. What brings you here? I hope you have not come with a problem for me to look into, for I must and shall be on this train."

"No, no, Mr. Holmes, you shall have your ocean voyage. I only came to see you off in the way of friendship, if I may presume so far. And, though there *are* those at Scotland Yard who would feel more comfortable if you were at hand whilst we're seeing to this Moriarty business, I believe we have it well enough in hand. It is only a matter of time before some of those fellows we have in custody decide to talk about their master, and, thanks to your work, we shall know where he is to be found."

"You expect Professor Moriarty to sit quietly in his den in the Victoria Docks to await your knock at the door, do you?" said Holmes.

Lestrade shrugged. "He is, of course, under constant watch. No person has left that place since your own departure, and I assure you that none will leave without one of my smartest detectives keeping close on his track."

"Are the river police also keeping watch? You will recall my mention of the trap door in the Professor's quarters."

Lestrade laughed heartily.

"Dear me, Mr. Holmes, you don't want to be getting fanciful! Dropping through a trap like a pantomime demon into a boat that spirits him away into the fog—that's more a scene for the magic show at Maskelyne and Devant's than what happens in real life, I can tell you! No, sir, it's the regular police work that does it in the end, be assured of that. I say, there's the guard signaling. You and Doctor Watson had best be getting aboard. I wish you both the finest of weather on your voyage!"

I could see the Inspector waving from the platform

as the train drew out of the station. Holmes looked back at him gloomily.

"There are times, Watson," said he, "when I feel a certain kinship with Professor Moriarty. With such guardians of the law as that, it seems almost criminal not to take advantage of the opportunity. You may depend upon it that, should the police ever gather the evidence they need, they will find their bird flown."

"*Floated* in this case, I should say," I put in, much pleased to have been able to correct Holmes' imagery.

He did not respond to the trifling jest, even with the irritation that such things sometimes roused in him, but stared out the window at the suburban landscape that now slid past us.

"What's going through your head, Holmes?"

When he spoke, it was more as though he marshalled his thoughts for his own benefit than made any effort to satisfy my curiosity.

"I am attempting to connect two events that by all sense and logic can*not* be connected—truly a futile exercise, Watson."

"What are they?"

"My conversation with Moriarty three nights ago, and the receipt of those shredded theater tickets this morning."

"But how could one have had the remotest connection with the other?"

"That is precisely it, Watson. I don't know . . . I don't know. And yet, were I Moriarty, and were my one unwavering determination the destruction of Sherlock Holmes, I would expend every effort at my command to discover the single, the only chink in his armor, however small it might be. And, once I had found it, if it exists at all, it is there I should thrust with all the strength and fury I could muster!"

I laughed heartily.

"Chink in *your* armor, Holmes? Rubbish! There's no such thing, man!"

He took out his pocket watch and snapped open the case, though it was too early in the journey to check on whether the train was keeping to its schedule. "Isn't there, Watson?" said he. "Isn't there? We must wait and see."

As Sherlock Holmes shut the watch and returned it to its pocket, I recalled that its inner lid bore a carefully cut and fitted miniature portrait of Irene Adler.

Chapter Three

The trouble with split-second arrangements is that *un*-split seconds have a way of adding up into minutes. An accretion of delays in our railway journey, no one of them significant in itself, came near in their sum to making us miss the *Pavonia*. Its tall stacks were already trailing smoke as the cab which had whirled us from the station clattered on to a nearly deserted pier. Porters, galvanized by the ten-shilling note I waved like a banner, trotted up the gangplank with our trunks, Holmes and I striding behind them.

I leaned against a rail, puffing slightly, I fear, with the exertion.

"We made it, Holmes, but only just," I said. "I don't know how we could have cut it any finer!"

Sherlock Holmes cocked his head toward the still-emplaced gangplank.

"Evidently one passenger has done so," said he.

I turned to look, and saw two burly fellows carrying an invalid-chair containing a black-swathed form, picking their way nimbly up the steeply angled board. A slighter young man in a dark frock-coat followed this strange entourage. As its bearers brought the chair on to the main deck, I caught a glimpse of a horridly emaciated, almost mummy-like face, with luxuriant, though unkempt, white hair straggling under the shawl which covered the head. Then the procession passed through a door to an inside corridor.

"Good Lord, Holmes!" said I. "I doubt that old lady's in any condition to stand five days at sea!"

"You forget, Watson, that the modern ocean liner

is as comfortable and well-appointed as any hotel in a great city—and a great deal more so, I fear, than most hospitals and rest-homes! In any case, you medical men are always talking of the marvelously revivifying effects of the ocean breezes. Doubtless she is counting on that. Though I must admit," he remarked, looking over the rail to the dark surface of the water below and wrinkling his nose, "that Liverpool Harbor seems to be another matter. Let us go below and see how to dispose our effects so that our shins, if not our tempers, survive the next six days!"

The *Pavonia* was well out into the Irish Sea by dusk, and Holmes sniffed the air with keen appreciation as we strolled on the deck.

"By Jove, Watson," said he, "this is a strange position for me to find myself in! I am on grave business, but can do nothing about it. Logic and deduction have taken me as far as they will; I have no way of being in touch with anyone on either side of the Atlantic to gain information or give instruction; I am, for very nearly the first time in my life, isolated and perforce inactive. Well, well, there it is—and I propose to make the best of it. It is a holiday I have not taken by choice, but a holiday nonetheless. I have not had much practice at it, but I believe I shall see what I can do about enjoying myself!"

In the event, Sherlock Holmes' recreation turned out not to be very different from his profession. His main delight, that first evening, was to observe his fellow-passengers as they promenaded, or were visible through the portholes of the several public rooms and saloons of the great liner.

"Why, it's a whole world, Watson, in minature! A throng of people going about their business, unthinking and uncaring of the genius and workmanship that constructed the vessel on which they travel, and scarcely more mindful of the perilous depths they traverse. Just so does the great globe itself plow through the ether, with its voyagers equally ignorant of its motive power."

"I believe the *Pavonia* has twin screws," said I, "and the engines are—"

He halted me with an impatient gesture, which he then amended to a friendly slap on the shoulder.

"Good old Watson," said he. "I can always count on you to deflate the hot-air balloon of my fancy when it gets too elevated! In any case, whether one considers the world or a ship, it matters not to me what makes it move; it is the passengers and their doings that provide the true fascination. And—hello—*is* that?—I do believe . . . Hum. Yes, Watson, *some* passengers are extremely interesting!"

I followed the direction of his gaze but saw nothing save a small group of men entering one of the saloons.

"Whom did you see, Holmes?" I asked.

"No one of any consequence," he responded. "I am, after all, on holiday, and life aboard ship must be considered in some sense like that of a water-hole in the veldt, where creatures normally inimical observe a truce, and even the lion and the jackal do not trouble one another."

The deck was almost deserted now, and Holmes turned to lean on the rail and observe the lights on the Irish coast slipping by.

This last glimpse of the shores of Europe, seen across the moonlit water, stirred me profoundly, but the air was keen and uncomfortably cool, and I felt the need of a sturdier covering than my tweeds. Holmes, as was his wont, was indifferent to the temperature, and I left him by the railing as I went below in search of my stoutest coat.

Picking my way down the corridor, in spite of myself tacking from wall to wall as the ship pitched in the waves, I stopped suddenly as I heard a familiar name spoken by a voice which seemed to come from nowhere. The sound was an eerie, distorted murmur, and I soon realized that it was some trick of the ventilating system that brought it to my ears. The speaker, or speakers, might be in any cabin on the corridor, and

I looked helplessly at the line of closed doors on both sides of it, filled with an urgency to know their location.

I could not swear to what I had heard, but it seemed to me to have been very like: *"Holmes, yes . . . he knew me . . . sure of it."* And then, in the same voice, or another: *". . . only way . . . deal with him immediately . . ."*

I stood irresolute for a moment. Had I heard aright? And even if I had, could there not be some innocent construction of that fragmentary exchange? I decided that, if there were, I could not think of it, and turned on my heel, meaning to seek Sherlock Holmes out and warn him of possible danger.

Unhappily, the corridors of the *Pavonia* provide many choices of direction at their intersections, and I had neglected to make myself master of their maze. It was only after several wrong turnings and some delay that I regained the main deck and hurried to where I had left Holmes—to see, as I approached the spot, a silent struggle between two shadowy figures!

Both were visible only in outline, a stocky shape of medium height contending with an unmistakably tall and lean form. And, as I watched, the taller shadow suddenly lurched violently over the railing and disappeared from sight.

"Holmes!" I cried out, in shock and sudden grief, and raced toward the spot. The other shape ran off into the darkness and was lost to sight.

I reached the railing and leaned over it, scanning the shimmering water in the vain hope of spying a floating form.

"There is no need to cry 'Man overboard!' just yet, Watson, and if you will lend me the strength of your arm for a moment, we may be able to avoid the necessity entirely."

Stunned, I looked down, and saw the glimmer of an upturned face below the edge of the deck. Then I made out two hands firmly clutching the bottom of the railing posts.

I made haste to draw Holmes up and assist him in his rather undignified scramble over the railing and on to the deck.

"What—what happened, Holmes?"

"I was taken by surprise and as nearly as anything pitched into the sea," he answered. "That much is clear. The motive is not, and I find it is a subject on which I should be glad to inform myself."

I recounted to him the fragmentary conversation I had heard, or half heard, in the corridor, and my apprension—amply justified, in the event—that it portended danger to him.

"Holmes, do you suppose some of Moriarty's men—?"

"No, no, Watson. This has the earmarks of an attack made in panic or on impulse, and the Professor's men do not allow themselves such failings. What you overheard, unfathomable as it was to you, makes it all clear to me now. As my assailant—whose name, address, and degraded habits I could easily give you if they would mean anything to you—undoubtedly supposes me dead, I think I shall allow myself to stage a resurrection for his benefit."

I followed in his steps as he strode off toward the nearest of the ship's many public rooms, dubious. What Holmes said was usually true, yet, with one murderous attack on him before the *Pavonia* was fairly at sea, it seemed imprudent to ignore the possibility that, by a means I could not grasp, one or more agents of the Professor had made their way on to the ship and meant to pursue their designs on him.

He peered briefly into one room and withdrew; then, another. In the doorway of the third, he stiffened and drew me quietly inside.

"That empty table over there will do us nicely, Watson. Do you stay to my left just a bit as we approach. Our quarry is at the next table, and it would be best for me to screen you."

I wondered that my friend could think me more recognizable than himself. Then I saw that, without the aid of the devices which made him a master of disguise, he altered, without in any way seeming unnatural about it, his general appearance with a slouching stride, a slump which took inches from his height, and one hand, raised as if to adjust his tie, which contrived to conceal the greater part of his face.

"The point, Watson," he murmured, "is to introduce enough unexpected and discordant elements into your walk, stance, and manner so that a possible watcher who has formed his image of you from the sum of those things will register a different impression entirely. A second glance would bring about recognition, but the great thing is not to occasion that second glance."

We reached the table, partly screened from its neighbor by a spiky kind of fern in a pot, and seated ourselves so that we might observe without being observed.

The nature of the activity at the next table was clear: a party of four men were preparing for a game of cards. One was a sleekly dressed and carefully combed man with a saturnine, predatory countenance. Another was an open-faced, burly young chap who seemed unused to the gaiety and luxury of the ship. The remaining pair appeared to be solid, unremarkable men of business, though evidently prosperous.

"I'm powerfully obliged to you gentlemen for asking me to join you in a little diversion," observed the young man in accents which I had no difficulty in recognizing as those of rural America. "A sea trip can be lonely without something to pass the time. And, say! I don't mind telling you I've enough in my poke to back up my play."

I saw the predatory-faced man dart a glance at him as he began to shuffle the cards.

I could follow the play easily enough, but soon grew restive and stirred in my chair. Holmes motioned me to silence with an impatient gesture.

"There will be drama enough in this in a moment or so, Watson," he whispered.

And so it proved. As the sharp-faced man drew in his winnings from the second hand played, the young American, at that point the major loser, sprang to his feet.

"See here!" he complained. "That jack wasn't in your hand when it was dealt—for here's the same one in mine!"

"Do you accuse me of cheating, sir?" said the winner in a blustering tone.

"Make of it what you will!" the American said, his face flushed. "I see what I see, and I'll not back down!"

The saturnine man's eyes shifted uneasily to the other two players, who returned his gaze sternly.

"You are mistaken, sir," he announced with a marked lack of conviction. "But be that as it may, I do not care to play further with you. Good evening to you!"

He pushed back his chair, rose and strode off.

"It seems as though you have saved us from an expensive lesson at the hands of a card sharp," ventured one of the businessmen. "He seemed unusually lucky, but I doubt if I or my friend would have spotted what was taking place."

"Where I come from, you have to keep an eye out for crooked play," said the American. "I've no use for such fellows, hate 'em like poison. In some of the places I've been, a man like that would be shot like a dog. Honest cards, honest dealing, honest play—that's my motto, and Uncle Sam's, too."

The game resumed, with the young man and his two companions now on the friendliest of terms.

Holmes watched keenly for a moment, then said loudly, though appearing not to address anyone in particular, "Wot price the briny, eh, Napper? Sweeter nor a cell in Wormwood Scrubs, cor strike me if it ain't."

His voice was a precise imitation of the hoarse croak of a seasoned convict, used to speaking from the corner of his mouth to elude the warders' notice.

The young American sprang from his seat, his ruddy face suddenly ashen. Without a word to his astonished companions, he left the table and made as if to dash for the outer door. As he passed our table, Holmes reached out an arm and drew him to a halt.

"On your way to a swim, Napper, like the one you tried to give me not an hour ago? I doubt you'd like it. Now, I don't propose to take steps about that trifling matter; a man's likely enough to see red when he runs into the man who got him four years' hard labor—was it four or five, Napper?—and give way to a touch of pique. But you've got that out of your system now, and have also exhausted your passion for card-playing and traveling-company melodrama for the remainder of this voyage, I trust. In any case, I don't wish or expect to hear further from you. Do you take my meaning?"

The stocky young man, in whom I could now perceive a resemblance to the shadowy form I had observed in near-mortal struggle with my friend, let fall a stream of foulness from his twisted lips, in accents more redolent of an East End slum than of the American plains.

"I see you do. Be off with you, then—and I suggest that you and Nice Ned keep to your cabin for the remainder of your voyage, or my patience may not prove to be all-enduring."

The "American" stumbled off, as unsteady in his steps as a blind man. The two businessmen, alarmed and confused, made their way to another part of the saloon.

"What on earth was all that, Holmes?" said I. "I was sure that that frank-faced young chap had exposed a card cheat, whom I supposed to be the man you were observing. But that seems not to be the case."

"That, Watson, was the Nottingham Napper, who used to make quite a good thing out of appearing a bumpkin among the flasher London crowds; and his associate, Nice Ned, whose sinister appearance made him one of the less successful of confidence-men in town. It was the Napper's genius that suggested this be turned to their advantage, and that they play a drama in which Ned would be cast as the villain, and the Napper as the honest hero. He has now worked up an atrocious stage-American manner, which I am surprised to think would fool a child" (I bridled at this, but then subsided; after all, I had not committed myself to Holmes on the matter) "and uses it to great advantage. Had the game continued, those two mercantile gentlemen would certainly have found themselves a great deal poorer by morning, and yet completely unsuspicious of the honest-dealing young fellow they had enriched. For had he not, after all, detected the blatant cheat in their midst? Well, well, they have shot their bolt now, and I do not expect to be troubled with them again."

Chapter Four

Two days at sea is enough to give one the feeling that he has lived that kind of life for a very long time, and will continue to do so for an indefinite period. Hour by hour, one becomes more attuned to the ways of the sea and more removed from those of the land. Relaxation is one important element of this feeling, and so is, I must confess, boredom. It was with a certain amount of pleasurable excitement, then, that both Holmes and I became aware of the smoking-concert being organized by the purser for the third night out. A Cunard purser must be qualified to fill most of the diplomatic or intelligence posts any government offers, for the *Pavonia*'s seemed to be aware of the interests and capabilities of every First Class passenger. On that afternoon, he approached Sherlock Holmes and invited him to participate.

"After all, sir," he said, "your virtuosity on the violin is well-known, and I venture to say that you have your instrument with you."

Holmes admitted both to his ability and to the presence of his fiddle, and made only the feeblest of attempts to beg off performing.

"I shall be glad of the chance to give it a proper tuning," he told me, his manner a good bit less than convincing. "Without a little exercise, it will doubtless be woefully slack from the sea air by the time we reach New York."

"I dare say. The plain fact is, Holmes, that you are idle and restless, and want the chance to show off."

"And you, Watson, have your nose out of joint

because you were not asked to appear at the concert—I confess it."

I considered this, and finally nodded my head. "Well . . . I don't suppose I should have cut much of a figure reciting 'The Charge of the Light Brigade,' which is about my only concert turn!"

"Mr. Sherlock Holmes?" We turned and saw a tall man in his twenties crossing the deck toward us. "Say, could I talk to you about the concert this evening?"

Though, to my ear, his accent was twin to that of the fraudulent Napper's, Holmes appeared to accept him as a genuine American, and was soon in amiable conversation with him.

"You see, they've got me booked to sing some cowboy songs, things the range hands sing around the campfires, and I don't know's I'm so set on doing it solo. I hear you're going to be playing the fiddle just before me, and I wonder if you could kind of stay on and give me some kind of accompaniment."

Holmes shook his head.

"I pretend to some expertise on the violin, Mr.—"

"Mix. First name, Thomas. Though nobody uses it in full, much."

"—but having, many years ago, travelled in America and heard your country fiddlers, I know my limitations too well to try to compete with their spirited performance. I shall look forward to hearing your songs. Many such, I believe, contain the history of notable crimes of the past—which touches on my professional interest. You were, then, yourself a cowboy?"

Mix shrugged.

"Have been. Got to know horses that way. Served in Cuba in 'ninety-eight, with the cavalry, then joined up with your army in South Africa."

"You were with Kitchener and Roberts?" said I, excited to meet a participant in that epic struggle, American though he might be.

"The generals didn't trickle down to my level much,"

he observed. "But yes, I was there—at Ladysmith, for one."

It seemed an odd thing to me that this ingenuous youth should have been engaged in a battle which had made history for the Empire, and I said, "Even though a foreigner, you must have been thrilled at our victory."

He gave me a squinting look.

"Well, Kruger's army's out of it now," said he, "but the war's not over. And the way it's going on is one reason I left. 'Mopping up' is what the dispatches call it, but it's fighting against the farmers on their farms, getting backshot from behind a *koppie,* burning people out of their homes, and herding old men, women, and children behind barbed wire so's you can keep an eye on 'em all in one place . . . What do the staff fellows call 'em, now— Oh, yes, 'concentration camps.' It's a pretty-sounding name, but it don't look so pretty when you see it."

I was not well-pleased to hear this sort of pro-Boer sentiment from one who, though he had admittedly been on the scene, did not have the instinctive viewpoint from which to understand these matters. Holmes divined my irritation, and attempted to compose matters by saying:

"Mr. Mix comes from a land which established itself little more than a century ago by just such a struggle. Whatever the deeper significance of the conflict, an American is bound to have a feeling for embattled farmers."

He turned to Mix and said, "I am always glad to meet an American, and, in spite of the business which brings me on this trip, happy to renew my acquaintance with your country. Your rebellion against the Crown was a sad loss to us, but I believe we have been the gainer by seeing the old English spirit of Liberty reborn in even stronger form. It would be a grand thing, would it not, if one day our two nations, in a time of greater understanding, might rejoin and truly form what your Constitution calls 'a more perfect union.' "

As always, when mounting one of his few abstractly philosophical hobby-horses, Holmes was close to being feverishly animated.

"We have the age and experience of Empire," he went on—almost declaiming—*"you,* the generosity and vigor of youth. Should Britain and America have been united two years ago, for instance, I doubt that this unhappiness in South Africa would ever have taken place—for who can imagine America exerting its might to force its will on a distant, poor nation of peasants, whatever the cause?"

Mix bent on him the same quizzical look he had at first given me. "When you get to the States," said he quietly, "you might look up old Geronimo. He and you could have a right interesting talk on that point. See you at the concert tonight, gentlemen."

I had to admit, as I sat in the lounge that night, that Mix's songs, delivered in a pleasant, slightly nasal baritone, were simple and affecting, dealing with star-crossed lovers, the work of cattle ranching, and duels on fine points of honor, set to tunes that mostly seemed English or Irish. My neighbor, a red-faced man in a rumpled dinner jacket, seemed much moved, and tears rolled down his cheeks.

Because of a change in the original order, Holmes was next to appear; and, though I had become inured to his abstracted scraping on his instrument during those times when he was brooding on some case—or the lack of any case—I responded to the richer tones and more assured performance that he now gave with enthusiasm. He eschewed the severely classical, and played several warmly haunting tunes reminiscent of Austria (lilting waltzes and pyrotechnic Gypsy melodies), though finishing, for reasons which escaped me, with "Drink to Me Only with Thine Eyes."

As the last strains of Holmes' violin died away,

the man next to me muttered, "Beau'f'l song. Swee'st song ever..."

I looked at him sharply. His eyes were glassy and through his open mouth his breath came raspingly. He was clearly quite drunk or under the influence of some opiate, and I felt a professional obligation to see him in surroundings where he could avoid further injury to his system.

"Why don't I see you to your cabin, old fellow?" I said as heartily as I could.

"Goo' idea. Hot ... here."

The man looked up at me as if through a pond-deep layer of water.

"And where's your cabin, eh? B Deck, or what?"

It seemed to me that he muttered "flummery."

"What?"

He made a greater effort for clarity.

" 'Nn ... frm'ry. Infirm'ry. 'M doctor. Ship's doctor."

I flushed with rage and shame for my profession. The one physician available for hundreds of souls on this ship, and the man was dead drunk! Brusquely, I helped him to his feet and ushered him from the lounge—aware, with little regret, that I was missing a large lady beginning an impassioned reading from her favorite poems of Ella Wheeler Wilcox.

Once we were out of earshot of the crowd and I was hustling him down the corridors and stairways that led to the infirmary, where he was quartered, I could not refrain from remonstrating with him.

"This is disgraceful, man! Think of those dependent on you—scores and scores of people who might at any moment suffer injury or sickness, and have only you to turn to! Why, there's an old lady aboard practically on the point of death! Do you propose to minister to her, should she require it, fuddled with drink? Or are you even aware of her presence among your ... *practice*?"

"Rum ol' lady," he mumbled, his rubber-legged walk making him twist in my grasp. "Of course saw 'r. She's sick. Tha's what I do, see sick people. Ship's doctor, y'know. Looked in on 'r jus' before concert, dam' fellow there wouldn't let m' see 'r. Gave me a cup of tea, chat 'bout how she's restin' com'f'bly, sent me off with flea in ear. I know that kin'. Next thing, 'll want death stifk't. No queshions 'n' a nice sea burial. Won't get it, not f'm me . . ."

During this drunken maundering, I managed to get the doctor to his quarters, place him on his bunk, and loosen his tie. Praying that there would be no calls until at least morning—preferably not until the end of the voyage—on his skills, I left him.

Outside the infirmary, I stood uncertainly for a moment.

The old lady I had seen carried on board was surely gravely ill, and the doctor who should have been responsible for her care was incapable of seeing to it. Ought I not make some effort to satisfy myself of her condition? If so, how? I had no idea of her name or her cabin, and I shrank from making inquiries of the ship's staff, which would inevitably expose the doctor to a ruinous investigation; after all, this might be only a momentary aberration, and, in spite of my indignation, I had no wish to destroy the man's career.

My problem was partially solved by the sudden appearance of a man whom I recognized as he who had followed the old lady's invalid-chair up the gangplank at Liverpool. He was emerging from a door down the corridor. He carried a book in one hand, and I surmised that he was going to the ship's library to exchange it for another, doubtless his means for whiling away the hours of his vigil.

"Sir!" I called after him.

He stopped, and I explained that I was a physician and—stretching the truth somewhat—had been asked to give a consultant's opinion on the old lady, about whom the ship's doctor was concerned.

"My aunt is well enough," the man observed. "She is sturdier than she looks, Doctor, and may well bury many who are younger than she." He seemed to find the thought amusing. "In any case, she has a passion for privacy, and flatly refuses to see any physician or other person whatever. You may tell your colleague that Miss Jacobs is as well as her age allows her, and that she does not stand in need of his services—or yours, sir. Good night."

I was affronted at the man's curtness, but, I confess, relieved that there seemed to be no further action which duty required of me. I made my way to the lounge for the remainder of the concert.

It seemed both an age and no time at all until we were standing past the statue of Liberty Enlightening the World in New York Harbor and making our way up the North River. On our left, a jumble of docks and warehouses marked our landing place; on our right, the awe-inspiring towers of Manhattan rose from their rocky base and strained into the morning sky. The water was alive with craft of every kind, from ungainly ferries plying between New York and every shore facing it, through rusty steamers, square-rigged grain and cargo ships, pleasure ketches and yawls, to mighty ocean liners like the one which carried us steadily up river.

"I fancy not London itself offers such a show, Watson," said Sherlock Holmes as he surveyed the scene. "Yet it is changing. Ten years ago, or twenty, sail would have dominated it. Now, that is giving way to steam, and soon the tall masts that reach to the clouds will be gone, all gone. It is strange to think that in fifty or seventy-five years' time the inhabitants of New York will never see a sailing vessel from one year's end to the next . . . Where have we got to now, I wonder?"

With audible cries of command from the bridge and the clangor of the engine-room telegraph, the *Pavonia,* abetted by nudging tugboats, was slowly turning toward the western shore of the river.

"If we're docking, this must be Hoboken," said I.

Holmes looked at me sharply.

"Your logic is both rigorous and unassailable, Watson, but you have an uncanny way of making it seem that logic is not always the answer. However, we'd best get to our packing."

As we stood on the dock, surrounded by our trunks, waiting for the ferry which would convey us to the New York side of the river, I was pleased to see that the old lady in the invalid-chair did not seem to have taken any harm from her sea voyage. As she was borne down the gangplank, she looked no worse than when I had first seen her in Liverpool. And she was clearly getting special treatment, I saw.

"My word, Holmes, Miss Jacobs has a private boat to take her to Manhattan. See there, they're lowering her into that steam launch!"

"Ah, the chair-bound old lady. How do you come to know her name, my dear fellow?"

I recounted my bizarre experiences with the ship's doctor and the old woman's uncommunicative attendant.

"You are sure of all that, Watson?" Holmes said in great excitement. "Word for word—what the doctor said and what the ... nephew ... said?"

"I believe I am?"

"Fool!"

"Holmes!"

Sherlock Holmes clapped me on the back reassuringly.

"Not you, Watson, never you! *I* should have seen it, should have known it. A wrapped form, kept hidden from all view ... the one doctor with a right to investigate fed a cup of tea and *somehow* made suddenly incapable ... the quick exit via a private launch ... and, to cap it all, Miss *Jacobs!*"

I considered these elements, but could form no picture from them, and said so.

"Jacob is the Latin form of *James,* Watson. I tell you, I am as certain as I am of tomorrow's sunrise that Professor James Moriarty is even now in that launch, laughing at how he has crossed the ocean under our very noses!"

Striving to live up to Holmes' complimentary remark concerning my logical faculties, I felt obliged to demur.

"I shouldn't have thought Moriarty was that sporting, to give us a chance to catch on to him."

"He isn't, Watson. He left just enough of a trail so that I would know he was here, and not enough for me to catch him. He means me to be aware of his presence. And that means that, whatever the significance of those torn-up theater tickets, they somehow point to Moriarty. His web is spread in the streets of this great city, Watson, and we venture into it. Let us hope that we prove to be wasps—to rend it and destroy the spider that sits at its center—and not flies that will leave their lifeless husks enmeshed in it. Either way, the game is afoot!"

Not for the first time, I was struck by the thought that Holmes, for a supposedly passionless logician, had an unnerving poetic streak to him. I could have done without that vivid comment about the flies.

Chapter Five

Standing among our piled trunks and luggage on the pavement outside the ferry landing on the Manhattan side, I had a curious sense of double vision. From the very color of the sky to the pitch of the roof of the warehouses and dwellings and the costumes of the inhabitants, it was clear that I was in a foreign country. Yet the language about me, though couched in a variety of strange accents, *was* English, and the bustle of the debarking crowd, the huddle of hansoms and carriages awaiting passengers, and the general air of busyness were not so different from what might have been encountered in London. I suppose I had been expecting something as completely strange as the first sight of India and the Red Sea ports I had seen during my Army service had been to me, and said as much to Holmes.

"The railways, the telegraph, the telephone, and the fast steamer have knit the world ever tighter, Watson," said he. "If something is thought of on Tuesday in Paris, it is known in Berlin, London and New York on Wednesday, and an uniquely tailored suit which sees the light of day in Old Bond Street may well be observed in little more than a week adorning half a dozen saunterers on Broadway. In a few years' time, any large city will be in all important respects indistinguishable from any other, I fear."

"Well, I suppose it is to our advantage that the cabs are much the same," I remarked. "I'd best get ourselves and our trunks and bags into one."

I raised a hand and gestured. A hansom driver

whipped up his steed and brought his vehicle up to us, one wheel on the sidewalk causing it to tilt alarmingly.

"No, man, not you!" I called up to where he perched atop his cab. "Look at these trunks. There's no room for them and two men in a hansom!"

A well-dressed woman wearing an extravagantly wide-brimmed hat, and standing next to me on the pavement, said, "Handsome is as handsome does."

"I beg your pardon, madam?" said I. "I was referring to the cab—that two-wheeler there. Are they not called hansoms in this country?"

"Oh, yes. But I wasn't talking about the cab. You're handsome enough yourself, you know."

I blush to admit that I was about to try to reply sensibly to this odd comment until I saw Holmes fairly doubled over with laughter, supporting himself against a lamp post. In my defense, I can merely say that it seemed to me only polite to expect to accommodate to variations in manners and modes of speech between England and America. And certainly, the woman did not have the look of the sordid drabs who offer themselves in far too many quarters of our capital.

"Be off with you, miss," I said sternly. "We've no time for that."

I was conscious that what I said might have been better phrased.

Holmes, still chuckling, helped me superintend the loading of our effects into a four-wheeler which had come up to replace the hansom, and instructed the driver to take us to the Empire Theater.

"I can't imagine what she hoped for from a crowd of arriving passengers from the ferry," said I, still somewhat in a huff. "It stands to reason that they would all have some sort of immediate business elsewhere."

"Well, well, Watson, she is in a profession older than either of ours, and I suppose she knows her trade. And Americans have a reputation for get-up-and-go, of being born salesmen. I dare say many a businessman is persuaded to arrive ten minutes or so late to an appointment with some tale of a traffic block."

The high good humor which my discomfiture had occasioned lasted only a few moments, and a brooding, impatient look settled on Holmes' face as we proceeded through the crowded streets. Now that I was fully immersed in New York, I began to see it as more truly foreign in spite of its many resemblances to London. The streets were all straight, giving a curiously disconnected and blocky appearance to the massed buildings, which were uniformly modern—none I saw could have been more than a century old, though some, in their architectural detail, aped every period of the past from Egyptian to Gothic. The trams which coursed the major streets and avenues, some drawn by horses and some propelled, as I later learned, by cable snaking beneath the street, dashed along at a pace which would have done credit to a fire engine or an ambulance in London. The people, too, moved along far more briskly than Londoners, in the aggregate flowing like a swift-moving stream past such obstacles as organ-grinders, chestnut-vendors, and persons hawking strange machines, the nature of which I could not make out from our carriage.

In spite of our driver's efforts, our speed slowed as the traffic thickened about us, with other hacks, drays, pleasure carriages—even a few automobiles, though far more than I would have expected to see on a London street—vying for the advantage of position.

We were now heading eastward on a wide street lined with shop buildings, some of them many stories in height. I looked ahead, startled, and saw a curious construction much like an iron roadway, ahead of us, suspended some twelve or fifteen yards above the level of the street.

"Whatever is that, Holmes?" said I.

"Dat's de El," replied the driver, leaving me no wiser.

"The elevated railway, Watson," said Holmes—

and, even as he spoke, his explanation became unnecessary, as I could see a train of cars hastening at a great pace along the track, bizarrely sustained in the air.

We inched our way to a point just short of this aerial phenomenon, then came to what seemed to amount to a near-final halt: no carriage, wagon, or automobile around us was moving. The reason was apparent. Where the major cross street we were on, a north-and-south avenue running underneath the elevated railway, and another which ran diagonally to both, met, there was a giant hole in the ground, a scene of feverish activity in which pick-and-shovel-wielding laborers and ungainly machines chuffing steam joined.

"What's that?" I inquired of the driver.

"De subway, er it will be, when's dey finishes it."

Again, the answer, though in something close to English, did not enlighten me.

"An underground railway," said Sherlock Holmes, now clearly almost beside himself with impatience.

"They're only getting round to that *now?*" I asked in genuine surprise.

I could scarcely recall London without the Underground, and could in no wise imagine living there without it. So much for American get-up-and-go!

"Well," said I with some impatience, looking around at the congealed mass of vehicles which surrounded us, "if they put half the transportation up in the air, and the other half under ground, perhaps it will be possible to get around the streets at faster than a walking pace!"

"Hey! How do I get t'rough here?" the driver bawled to a workman in the excavation.

"You don't," came the reply. "Go back an' cut over to Seventh."

"Ah, dat'll take half an hour," the driver said in disgust.

Holmes consulted his watch.

"Half past three already, Watson! No, it won't do! Driver! Where are we now?"

"T'irty-fourt' Street, just about at Sixt' Avenue."

"And the Empire's at Thirty-ninth and Broadway. Come along, Watson, the walk will do us good." So saying, he pulled out some bills from his note-case and handed them up to the driver. "Get our things to the Hotel Algonquin as fast as you're able. I'm sure this will take care of your time and trouble." As I knew, from my hasty researches at the steamship office, that New York cab fares were an American dollar a mile for four-wheelers, and the same amount by the hour, it seemed to me that the sum Holmes tendered would have taken care of the hackman for the rest of the day.

"Come on, Watson," said Sherlock Holmes, stepping briskly from the carriage. "We've walked that distance tenfold in a single afternoon in London!"

"But not," said I, falling in with his stride, "picking our way among trenchworks worthy of a battlefield!"

For the subway excavation continued along the street on which we were walking, and we were obliged to skirt banks of upturned earth and rubble and sometimes make our way across a ditch on a kind of plank walk.

"Heads up!" cried a workman toiling away in the pit, and flung a shovelful of dirt into the air.

Only by skipping nimbly aside was I able to avoid receiving it full on my person. I allowed myself the peevish reflection that George the Third, had he undergone the experience of a New York traffic block and then been showered with earth, might not have made so much of a fuss about relinquishing his colonies. Part of my discomfort was due to the temperature, which seemed inordinately warm for the end of March, but then I recalled that New York lies at a considerably more southerly latitude than London, and is therefore by comparison nearly in the Tropics.

As we walked on, my spirits lifted. The shops, restaurants, theaters, and hotels which lined the street presented a scene of colorful activity, and the air, though warm, had in it a bracing tang new to me.

By keeping an eye on the street signs and noticing that the numbers became higher as we made our way northward, I was able at last to deduce that the next street we would come to was Thirty-ninth, our destination. On its corner I saw a massive building in elaborately carved brownstone, stretching from one street to the next.

"Good heavens, Holmes," said I. "Is that the Empire Theater? It dwarfs practically anything in London except the Albert Hall."

"No, Watson, it's the Metropolitan Opera House. The Empire's just around this corner."

We turned it, and I perceived the theater's identifying sign projecting into the street. Though not as grand as the opera house, it was still on a larger scale than most of our theaters, and evidently newly constructed.

I followed Sherlock Holmes into the lobby, grateful for its musty coolness after the heat of the streets.

Holmes pointed toward the brass-grilled ticket window and said, "Watson, just try to get us two tickets for tonight, will you? I'm going to try to find out what I can inside."

"Oh, yes, of course, Holmes," I responded. "I'll join you as soon as I'm done."

He pushed open the door leading to the theater auditorium and disappeared. I made my purchase without having to try to decipher the seating plan of the Empire, as the clerk offered me no choice.

"These are the last seats for tonight's performance, mister. They're good ones. I wouldn't have 'em except somebody returned 'em just an hour ago. Take 'em or leave 'em."

I took them, pleased at the fortunate happenstance that had enabled me to execute my commission, though the two and a half dollars—ten shillings—each seat cost seemed to me excessive. I turned to follow Holmes.

A glance at the tickets, however, made me stop,

staring, for an instant, and returned to the ticket window. After a brief exchange of questions and answers with the clerk, I left the lobby.

As I entered the rear of the theater, I saw Holmes down front, just commencing a conversation with a man in a rumpled jacket, evidently the stage doorman, who was emerging from behind the scenes.

"Yes, sir?" this fellow called.

"How do you do? Is Miss Irene Adler in the theater, do you know?"

"Nobody's here but me."

"I must see her at once! Can you tell me where I might reach her?"

The doorman shook his head.

"No one is to be disturbed before curtain time. Mr. Furman's orders."

"But this is extremely urgent!"

I slowed my steps and remained in the gloom at the back of the auditorium, feeling it best to let Holmes handle this problem without the extraneous factor of my presence.

"So are Mr. Furman's orders," the doorman said complacently.

Holmes persisted.

"Do you know her address?" he inquired.

The doorman moved to the edge of the stage and confronted Holmes.

"Look, I just finished telling you—"

"Yes, yes, quite," said Holmes testily. "Look here, my good man, when did you last see Miss Adler?"

"This morning, at line rehearsal."

Holmes stiffened, his next words freighted with eagerness.

"Was she all right?"

"Letter perfect."

"*Was* she? I can't tell you how relieved I am to hear you say so! Now, if I might prevail on you for a further service . . ." I saw him take out his note-case and pass up a bill and one of his calling-cards to the doorman. "Would you be so kind as to give Miss Adler my card directly when she gets here, and tell her that I am at the Algonquin Hotel and must speak to her as soon as possible?"

The doorman's eyes widened as he inspected the card, and he glanced sharply at Holmes.

"I guess I can do that for you, all right, Mr. Sherlock Holmes!"

I felt a small glow of pride at the thought that my modest chronicles of my friend's adventures had made his name famous and respected, even here.

"You shall have earned my eternal gratitude," said Holmes, and turned to walk up the aisle.

I moved to meet him, flourishing the theater tickets which had so perplexed me. The doorman, evidently not needed at his post while the theater was largely deserted, sank into a chair at the left of the stage and appeared to fall into that somnolence which men in tedious but inactive jobs learn to cultivate.

"I say, Holmes—" I began.

"Well, we've one bit of reassurance in any event," said he, as much musing to himself as sharing information with me. "As late as this morning she was apparently in good health. Now, Watson, what have you been able to accomplish?"

"It's a rum go, Holmes, a deucedly rum go. Look at these tickets—last two in the house for tonight, the chap at the window claims."

Sherlock Holmes' expression darkened as he took the slips of pasteboard from my hands and read the printing thereon.

"Row E, seats one and three—"

He whirled and made for the door leading to the lobby.

"Don't bother, Holmes," I told him. "I've already questioned the fellow."

"Have you, now?" said he, stopping and facing me once more.

"Yes. Those tickets were purchased a fortnight ago —by Irene Adler."

Holmes stared at me keenly, and nodded his head slowly. "To send to me."

"Exactly."

"Then how come they to be here?"

"They were returned."

"When, Watson?"

"Earlier this afternoon."

"And by whom?"

"Some stranger to the man in the ticket office. Never saw him before, he says. Holmes, what on earth do you make of it all?"

Even in the gloom of the theater, its only light the single glaring bulb dangling from a flex over the stage where the resting—or sleeping—doorman sat, I could see that Sherlock Holmes' face was stern and troubled.

"Watson," said he, "all my apprehensions are returning. Those tickets sent to Baker Street were forgeries. These, the genuine ones, were intercepted before they could reach me."

What he said seemed to follow from the known facts, but to make no sensible pattern.

"But whatever for?" said I.

Holmes folded his length into one of the narrow seats next the aisle and slumped in it, staring unseeingly at the rows of seat-backs in front of him.

After a moment, he said softly, "A phrase continues to ring in my ears, Watson: 'The crime of the century—the past century, this one, and all centuries yet to come—is now in preparation.' Moriarty said that to me."

"You think that he's behind . . . whatever it is that's going on?"

"'. . . it will take place before your very eyes! And you will be powerless to prevent it!' It smells of greasepaint, Watson, the bluster of a melodrama villain— yet Professor Moriarty is not the man to boast idly! I am nine parts certain that he's in New York at this very moment, and that this business with the tickets is his doing." He glanced up at me. "There's deviltry afoot, Watson. I feel it in my very marrow!"

"Well, what do we do about it?" said I.

Sherlock Holmes held up the tickets.

"Until it chooses to reveal its nature to us," he replied, "we can do nothing but dress, dine, and attend the theater this evening. Moriarty has all the strings, it seems, and when he pulls, we needs must caper. But each move he makes, I tell you, Watson, brings us closer to finding what drama he means us to play. And when we know that, I fancy we may provide him with a different last act than that he has written!"

He fairly sprang out of his seat and strode from the theater. I followed him, pondering on the dark and twisting path that lay ahead of us. That it led through perilous territory, I was sure; but the worst of it was that the shape of those perils was unknown.

I know now that, had I chanced to glance behind me as I made my way from the Empire Theater, I might have gained some inkling as to the reach of Professor Moriarty. I did not see what I now tell, but am satisfied that it is a true account of the events.

As the doors swung to behind us, the doorman rose from his seat, pulled a cloth cap from his pocket, and ran backstage, out the stage door and into the street, where he hailed a cab. Spurred by the promise of a double fare, the driver soon dropped his passenger in a mean district on the East River waterfront, as dismal and decrepit as a certain section of the Victoria Docks that has already figured in this narrative.

Slipping into a narrow space between two sagging, boarded-up buildings, the theater doorman rapped on a scarred door, which immediately opened to reveal a man in a tightly fitting, loudly checked suit.

"Is he in?" asked the doorman.

The man in the checked suit had no need to ask to whom the pronoun referred.

He gestured with his thumb, saying, "Upstairs."

The stage doorman scurried up the flight of stairs, knocked at a door, and opened it after hearing a brusque "Come in!"

Colonel Sebastian Moran, or any other of Professor Moriarty's minions now languishing in the Bow Street jail, would have paused a moment in astonishment upon entering the room. So might Sherlock Holmes. It was a replica, exact in every detail—except for its still-whole chandelier—of Moriarty's quarters in the Victoria Docks. The Professor, having found an arrangement that suited him, saw no reason not to have it available to him wherever he might be.

The doorman, being ignorant of this circumstance, took no notice of the room beyond his usual pang of envy at its richness. He did observe, with fleeting surprise, a woman's black dress and a straggling white wig tossed in a chair in the corner. He did not, even in his mind, speculate on their meaning; it didn't do to wonder about what *he* was up to.

"Do you have something for me, Zimmer?" said Moriarty.

The doorman held Holmes' card out to him. The banknote he had received, he decided, was not relevant to the Professor's purposes.

"He's here."

The Professor smiled broadly.

"Indeed he is . . ." He looked up at Zimmer. "All right, back to your post. You know what to do."

The doorman nodded and made a sketchy gesture akin to a salute, then turned and left the room.

Professor Moriarty leaned back in his chair, his pale face aglow with a satisfied look of the sort that, in years past, would have been elicited by the final working-out of a complex equation. He opened the top drawer of the desk, and slid out a folded sheet of thick paper: a playbill for the Empire for that evening. One spatulate fingertip touched the printed name of Irene Adler, almost caressing it.

"Act One," he murmured. "And, with the cast assembled . . . the play begins!"

Chapter Six

The walk to our hotel, unpacking and bestowing our belongings, freshening up and dressing for dinner, and dinner itself, occupied the remainder of the time until the curtain was due to rise at the Empire; and occupied it, I must confess, in spite of the apprehensions both Holmes and I entertained regarding the future, quite agreeably. Dr. Johnson is supposed to have said that life affords few greater pleasures than riding with a pretty woman in a post-chaise, but I submit that to be for the first time in a great foreign city on an early Spring evening, venturing forth in search of the best dining the place affords, with a major theatrical opening to follow, must come close to matching Johnson's ideal.

The very next street-corner to the west of our hotel, at Fifth Avenue, afforded two restaurants, Delmonico's and Sherry's. (It struck me as distinctly odd that New Yorkers could attach the same rich associations to their numbered thoroughfares as we do to our street names which speak of a thousand and more years of history, yet it must be so; for, to them, there is as much difference between Fifth Avenue and Ninth as we would perceive between Park Lane and Wardour Street.) I was at first attracted by the thought of Sherry's, as the name indicated that they had a civilized regard for that estimable drink, but the sign outside proclaiming that Mr. Louis Sherry had "Family and Bachelor Apartments to Rent," dissuaded me.

"After all, Holmes," said I, "if the man is concerned with providing accommodations, it follows that he has the less attention to give to the food he serves, and is in fact apt to set the sort of table one would expect at a superior lodging-house." I will defend the logic of my deduction, but must in fairness say that later experience persuaded me that Louis Sherry, in spite of taking in lodgers, deals most estimably with those who dine in his establishment.

In any case, Delmonico's proved to be an excellent choice for our first evening in New York. A white limestone building rising some six floors above the street level, and dominating its near neighbors, it had the aspect of a Renaissance palace, viewed from the outside. Once entered, it offered the alternatives of the Palm Room, a dining-room in the Louis XIV style, an oak-wainscotted café, and an upstairs dining-room that afforded a view down Fifth Avenue.

The airy, yellow-and-white color scheme of the Palm Room seemed the most attractive to me, and, as Holmes was, as nearly always, indifferent to his surroundings, I settled upon it. I suppose that London may provide scenes of greater elegance and luxury in its great hotels and restaurants, but the plain fact is, I was not much acquainted with them, my association with Sherlock Holmes tending to steer me toward a hastily downed cup of tea and a bun in an A.B.C. shop while we prowled the streets after a miscreant—a well-grilled sole at Simpson's in the Strand representing the height of our culinary adventures at home.

At Delmonico's, the bill of fare seemed half as tall as a man, and I confess that I rather let myself go in sampling it: some oysters Rockefeller to start, then a cold soup, a portion of an exotic fish known as red snapper, for the game course a nicely done piece of venison . . . A full account of that repast would both impede my narrative and, I fear, establish me as a glutton in the reader's eyes, so I shall stop near the beginning. Holmes, never one to appreciate much what he ate, so long as it was ample and fresh, contented himself with beef and potatoes.

Half an hour before curtain-time, we left the restaurant and entered on to the brightly lit avenue, even at this hour crammed with cabs, coaches, drays, and omnibusses—I was glad that at least on this one thoroughfare, the speeding trams were not in evidence. With the theater just about half a mile away, Holmes suggested that we walk to it, and I acceded enthusiastically. After doing myself so well at Delmonico's, I felt that I needed some exercise before preparing to wedge myself into a theater seat for a period of two hours or so.

As it turned out, I need not have been concerned, either about a long period spent sitting in the theater, or lack of exercise.

When we took our two fifth-row seats just off one of the aisles, it lacked five minutes to the stated curtain-time. Ten minutes later, the curtain remained down, and I had become tired of glancing around at the glittering assembly that filled the Empire, a crowd that gave far more of an impression of both opulence and raw vigor than do our London theatergoers.

I observed Sherlock Holmes take out his watch, open the case, and glance inside.

"Time they were getting on with it, eh, Holmes?" said I.

He gave me a quick look and remarked, "I hadn't noticed the time, Watson—but, yes, I do believe you're right. It's five minutes past time now, and no sign—"

He cast a worried frown toward the stage, and I was left to wonder why he might have been looking inside his watch if not to see what time it told.

As the moments passed, a buzz rose from others in the audience who were concerned or irritated by the delay. Then the murmurs rose to a peak and were stilled as a worried-looking man in a dinner jacket entered from the wings and strode to the center of the stage, holding up both hands in a gesture beseeching silence.

"That's Furman, the producer," I heard a man in front of me mutter to his neighbor.

"Ladies and gentlemen," the man on stage called, his voice quavering in evident nervousness. "I ask your indulgence, please!" Next to me, Holmes stirred uneasily. "Due to the sudden indisposition of Miss Irene Adler—"

Holmes was on his feet in an instant, fairly wrenching me out of my seat with a painful grip on my arm.

"Watson! Quick!" said he, and set off down the aisle. I followed him, and turned with him to race across the space in front of the first row, seeing the astonished faces of the theater patrons flicker past me. From the stage above, I could hear Furman continuing his explanation to the audience.

"—the role of Paula will be played at this performance by Miss May Robson. Thank you."

Exclamations of surprise and disappointment were just beginning to rise from the crowd as we pushed through the exit door and pounded along a short corridor and up a flight of stairs that led us to the wings.

Furman was now standing there, watching the opening scene of the performance. Somewhat behind him, I noticed the doorman with whom Holmes had conversed that afternoon.

"I demand to be taken to Miss Adler at once! My name is Sherlock Holmes!"

I had half expected the producer to be affronted at this unceremonious and assertive introduction, but Furman's eyes widened, and he grasped the lapels of Holmes' tailcoat as a drowning man might hold to a life-preserver.

"Mr. Holmes, thank heaven you're here!" said he.

"Where is she?"

"So far as I know, at home."

"I must know *exactly* what has happened," said Holmes.

Furman wiped his glistening brow, and replied, "All I can tell you, sir, is that when she didn't appear after the half-hour call, I sent the call boy to her house."

"And?"

Furman produced an envelope from an inner pocket of his jacket.

"He returned with this."

"Let me see it!" Holmes demanded, although, as he twitched it from Furman's grasp as he spoke, his words were unnecessary.

He removed from it a folded sheet of paper and scanned it rapidly.

"As you see," said Furman, "all it says is that she is ill and cannot perform." His hands clenched and unclenched, as if looking for something solid to grasp. "With the house already full—*and* for the first time this season, darn it!—and the curtain already delayed fifteen minutes, I had no alternative but to go out front and make the announcement you just heard. Mr. Holmes, can you shed any light on such behavior? It's absolutely unlike Miss Adler!"

"I can shed *some* light on it, Mr. Furman," Holmes replied somberly. "This note—it was not written by a person suddenly taken ill. In such a case, there might well be signs of weakness, though the writing would be formed with all the more care to compensate for that. But this—the hasty scrawl, showing that the hand shook so that it was scarcely able to hold the pen . . . And here—here—and here—the pen has actually dropped from her hand! I have seen such missives in the past, sir, and I tell you that this letter was written by someone in the clutches of extreme terror! Mr. Furman, I must have Miss Adler's address at once!"

Furman was pale, and his eyes registered dismay and fear.

"It's number four, Gramercy Park West, but—"

"This is no time for 'buts,' Mr. Furman! Four, Gramercy Park West! Come, Watson!"

Sherlock Holmes turned on his heel and made for the stage door, with myself in hot pursuit. I was for an instant somewhat surprised not to see the stage doorman at his post, but supposed that he was mingling with the stagehands in the wings, eager to pick up gossip about what had happened.

A rattling ride in a hansom brought us to our destination in not much above five minutes. I do not know whether it was the extra money Holmes promised for speed, or the electric sense of urgency about him that galvanized our Jehu. We stepped from the cab to find ourselves on a quiet street that might have been a London square: a row of narrow houses fronting a lamplit park surrounded with an iron grill. Number four was a house much like its neighbors. I paid the cabby the fare Holmes had promised, while my friend bounded up the broad steps, the tails of his coat streaming behind him, and vigorously rang the bell beside the front door.

As I came up the steps behind him, the door opened, and a tall man in dark jacket and striped trousers stood in the doorway.

"Yes, sir?" said he.

"Miss Irene Adler, if you please, at once!"

The man, doubtless the butler, unless they were called something else in this country, stiffened and said, "I'm sorry, sir. Miss Adler is not at home to—"

Sherlock Holmes pushed past him; I followed, and we found ourselves in a small foyer, simply but elegantly appointed. Holmes turned to confront the indignant butler, who seemed ready to try conclusions with him.

"Not at home—to Sherlock Holmes? I must have *that* assurance from the lips of the lady herself! Step aside, my man!"

He turned toward the interior of the house and called loudly, "Irene! Are you here?"

"I am here, Sherlock!"

We looked toward the head of a flight of stairs leading down to the foyer, and I beheld, above a peach-colored peignoir that wrapped her form, the face of Irene Adler—scarcely changed, as far as the soft lamplight in the room could let me discern, from the way she had looked on that occasion, so many years past, when she had triumphed in the dangerous game she had played with Holmes. I found myself exchanging a glance of surprise with the butler. For myself, it was a distinct shock to hear my friend addressed by his first name; I had never done so, and had never heard anyone else employ it. As far as the butler was concerned, it was a clear signal that his defensive tactics would not be needed, and he relaxed perceptibly, though with a fleeting look of disappointment.

"It's all right, Heller," Irene Adler called. "Mr. Holmes and Dr. Watson may come in."

"Yes, madam," the butler answered stolidly.

Very gravely, with measured pace, Holmes walked up the stairs toward where Irene Adler stood. I followed. As he reached her, she turned to face him.

"In here," she said, and walked through an archway leading into a drawing-room.

It was the first domestic interior I had seen in New York, and I surveyed it with interest—partly occasioned by the fact that Sherlock Holmes was examining every aspect of it as keenly as though it had been the scene of a crime he had been called upon to investigate.

Three tall windows fronting on the square were covered with drapes made of a kind of velour stuff. In a brick fireplace topped with a wooden mantel, a banked coal fire burned slowly but steadily. The usual furniture of the room of a cultivated person was here, little different from what I might have expected to find in a similar establishment in the West End of Kensington, though I had the vague sense that something about it reminded me of a stage set—a certain unused look to the plump cushions and soft chairs. Though that, I supposed, was natural enough, considering Irene Adler's profession. I could not see what there was to arouse Holmes' obvious attention.

"May I ring for some refreshments?" said Irene Adler, cool and composed as any hostess receiving invited guests, not at all indicating that she was speaking to two middle-aged gentlemen who had burst in upon her and (one of them, at least) shoved her butler aside and bawled a peremptory demand for her presence. "Coffee? Brandy? Would you care to sit down? You're looking quite well, Sherlock. You've hardly changed in the years since last we met. Dr. Watson, are you quite well also?"

I was about to reply that I was, without going into any particulars of my health, although I was aware of a certain shortness of breath which might have resulted from the excellent dinner at Delmonico's, when Holmes forestalled me.

"We were at the theater tonight," said he.

Irene Adler stood as still as a statue. "Did the performance go on?"

"With your understudy. The audience, of course, were disappointed at the substitution."

"Miss Robson is a very promising young performer."

"What is this 'indisposition' from which you are suffering?"

Holmes' tone left no doubt that he was little inclined to credit the existence of such an illness, and, indeed, I myself could detect no sign of any malady in the splendid, though somehow constrained, woman who stood before us.

"A trifling matter, really. I'll be quite all right in a matter of—"

"Irene!" Holmes' voice, deep and harsh, seemed wrenched from his very depths, and Miss Adler stepped back from him, as if shaken by its force. *"Why* did you not go to the theater tonight?"

She could not meet his gaze, and her voice came in faltering tones.

"I . . . I . . . Didn't Mr. Furman explain that I was—?"

"I insist that I be spared this masquerade! It demeans a friendship of almost ten years' standing!"

Sherlock Holmes' words and manner were dramatic enough for the scene, but I found myself as much fascinated by the change I saw in him as by the drama that was going forward. I had seen my friend in a variety of moods, and in the grip of many kinds of emotion in the course of my association with him: a savage exultation at bringing to book some particularly vile criminal; regret and mourning at the fate of a victim which a turn of luck might have prevented; deep concern, once, when it seemed that I had been gravely wounded; morose despair when one of his private fits of depression was on him. Yet this vigorous urgency, which seemed somehow the attribute of a younger and less cerebrally-inclined man, was new to me.

He continued in the same vein, giving a stern nod in response to her anxious look.

"Yes! It's time for the truth, Irene! What is it that holds you in the grip of almost unbearable terror? What message are you awaiting, and why are you prepared to remain up the entire night—and not leave this house until you receive it?"

I blinked, wondering, in spite of my long familiarity with his methods of deduction, how he had arrived at this conclusion. There certainly seemed nothing anywhere I could see to sustain it.

Irene Adler, however, did not trouble herself with that sort of question, and gave a short, harsh laugh with a high pitch to it I didn't like the sound of.

"I should have remembered," she said. "One cannot pretend in front of Mr. Sherlock Holmes!"

Her tacit confirmation of what her inquisitor had said bewildered me.

"Yes, but look here, Holmes," said I. "How did you know about—what was it?—a message. Staying up all night? Not leaving the house? Surely—"

"It's simplicity itself!" Holmes seemed to find relief in reverting to his long-established custom of making things clear to me, and for the moment virtually ignored Irene Adler, whose gaze remained bent steadily upon him. He strode to the centermost of the three windows fronting on Gramercy Park, and pointed to the drapes that concealed it. "This curtain hangs un-

tidily. Again and again, someone has thrust it aside
—like this—so that the street below— Aha! The windows
leading out on to the balcony—which I am sure
you noticed, Watson, as we entered the house—are
unlatched!"

He flung open the center window, which I could
now see was more like a glass-panelled door, and
stepped onto the balcony.

"As I say," he continued, "someone has repeatedly
stepped out here to look in all directions! Waiting.
Waiting for *what?*"

Holmes stepped back into the room and continued
his exposition. A sweeping gesture took in the chairs
and cushioned sofa.

"Not a single piece of furniture in this room shows
the imprint of a human form! Irene, you have spent
the time since at least eight tonight pacing this floor,
sitting *only* at that desk in the corner to write your
note to Mr. Furman! Ah! What's this?"

His aquiline nose seemed almost to sniff the air as
if picking up the scent of crime as he strode to the sofa
and lifted up a framed picture lying on its face. Turning
it over, he gazed at it long and inquiringly.

Determined not to distract him, but consumed with
curiosity, I made my way to Holmes' side and had a
look for myself. It was a sepia-toned photograph of a
boy of some nine years of age, thinner of face, perhaps,
than a healthy lad ought to be, yet with an
appearance of vigor and an inquiring cast of countenance.

"Who is this child?" said Sherlock Holmes.

Irene Adler was silent for a moment, then said
evenly, "His name is Scott. He is my son."

I stirred uneasily. As a doctor, I have seen much of
the unconventional side of life—and much more of it
as a result of joining Holmes in his work—and I am
also aware that Mr. Bernard Shaw and Herr (if that
is how Norwegians style themselves) Ibsen have in
their work raised flouting of the conventions to the
status of a positive moral duty. Yet I felt distinctly

awkward at hearing *Miss* Irene Adler speak of her son.

Holmes looked sharply at her and then back to the picture.

"Where is the boy now?" he inquired.

"He is . . . upstairs. In bed." Irene Adler appeared to be looking intently at a point on the wall considerably to Holmes' left.

"May I see him?"

"He is asleep."

"I shall be *very* quiet." Something of his old sardonic manner was creeping back into the detective's tone.

Irene Adler was silent for a moment, and Holmes' lips thinned in an almost mocking smile.

She sighed deeply and said, "I am afraid I cannot oblige you."

Holmes nodded.

"I am convinced that you cannot!" he said.

He looked at her keenly for a moment, then turned and walked to the delicate writing-desk that stood against one wall. He bent over it, nodded his head, and ran a finger along one corner of the top. As he straightened from his crouching position, Irene Adler's eyes were on him, wide with fear.

"That photograph ordinarily stands here on this desk," said Holmes. "A faint line of dust marks where its base usually rests." He walked slowly back to where the woman stood, holding the framed picture up. "You seized it up while you were pacing, didn't you? I can see you . . . holding it, casting a longing, anxious look upon it, even giving way to a sob of anxiety—and then flinging it to the sofa!"

He performed the same action as he spoke, and the picture spun through the air to land in the same position in which I had first noticed it.

"The boy is *not* upstairs in bed, Irene! The boy is not in this house at all! The boy has been *kidnapped!*"

Irene Adler raised two clenched fists and struck at

his snowy shirt front, not as if attacking him but as if in a frenzy that demanded some physical expression.

"Yes! Yes, yes, yes! He *has* been kidnapped, and I am out of my mind with grief and terror!"

Chapter Seven

I started toward Miss Adler in alarm, saying "Holmes! Great heavens, man, the lady's at the end of her tether!"

Holmes snapped, "Watson, fetch some brandy!" then grasped her firmly by the upper arms and looked at her with an intensity that was almost ferocious. "Irene, get hold of yourself!" said he. "We have no time! I must know precisely what happened."

She seemed on the verge of struggling in his grasp, then relaxed and looked up at him with a calmer expression. Her voice was even when she spoke.

"Yes, yes, of course."

Holmes opened his hands and dropped them to his sides. Irene Adler stepped away from him, went to the tasselled bell-pull that hung down one wall, and tugged it once.

"The brandy's on the sideboard, Dr. Watson, in the decanter. I will have a drop, thank you."

"Of course, my dear lady. Of course, of course!"

I poured out what I judged to be a medicinal doze of the liquor into a crystal balloon glass that stood next to the cut-glass decanter; enough to relax the tension that was fairly tearing her apart, not so much as to dull her wits. Its aroma proclaimed it to be of excellent quality, but now was not the time for either Holmes or myself to sample it; it looked as though we should need the clearest of heads, even the tightest-strung of nerves, in order to see this ominous business through.

I handed Irene Adler the glass, and she took a sip.

I could see her relax perceptibly, as much, I judged, from the realization that her dread secret was now shared and that she was to have the help of Sherlock Holmes (and John Watson, though I doubted that my presence weighed very heavily in the balance with her) as from the warming effect of the brandy.

Summoned by the bell, Heller, the butler, entered through the archway.

"Yes, ma'am?" said he.

"Heller," Irene Adler asked him, "will you . . . will you ask Frau Reichenbach to come down right away, please?"

"Of course, ma'am."

He turned and left, moving with the deft silence characteristic of his calling. Apparently even American butlers cultivate the ideal of appearing to operate like well-oiled machinery.

"Frau Reichenbach is . . . ?" said Sherlock Holmes.

"It was she who was with Scott when he . . ." Irene Adler took another sip of the brandy. "She is the boy's governess."

She could scarcely have been mistaken for anything else, when, moments later, she stood just inside the archway and gave her account of the events of the afternoon. Her severely starched uniform, the hair pulled into a tight bun atop her head, the stiff stance with hands folded in front of her, the immobile face and light-blue eyes bespoke both her occupation and her nationality. I judged her age to be not far past thirty.

I had allowed myself to sink into a comfortable wing-chair. Irene Adler was seated on the sofa, still holding the brandy glass. Holmes paced back and forth as he questioned Frau Reichenbach.

"I had gone to meet the young boy at school," said she in a marked German accent, "and we were walking home, which we do each day."

"You're referring to this afternoon, Frau Reichenbach?"

"*Ja.*"

"Describe what occurred, please."

"Three blocks from here, maybe four—we were coming up Twentieth Street—a carriage drew up beside us and stopped. A man was on top, driving a horse. It was a closed carriage and all the shades were down. A man leaped out of the inside . . ." She faltered in her speech.

"Yes? Go on, please!"

"He seized and kicked me!"

I was shocked.

"Good heavens! The brute!" said I.

"Watson, please! Seized and kicked you, Frau Reichenbach?"

The governess nodded vigorously.

"First by the hair, like this!" She tugged mightily at the knot of it on top of her head, in demonstration. "And then with the foot, like this!" She lashed out with the pointed, polished toe of her shoe, and added a comment which momentarily startled me: "In the chin!"

It seemed a bizarre method of attack, but a second's thought gave me the probable solution.

"I expect she means the shin, Holmes. That would be—"

"*Do* you think so, Watson? Thank you so very much."

The tone in which he said this, though of an almost exaggerated politeness, left me in no doubt that, as usual, he preferred to conduct his interrogation without interpolations, however helpful.

Holmes turned back to the governess.

"What happened then?"

"He threw me into the gutter—*Gott im Himmel*, was he strong!—then laid his hands on the boy and dragged him into the carriage! Then away they raced before it could be said *Donner und Blitzen!*"

"Did you mark which way they went? Do you recall any particular features of the carriage?"

"*Nein*. I was in my head confused and also in the

gutter lying. When I stood and looked, there was nothing."

"And then?"

"I hurried here, in spite of my bruises and the pain in my leg, the dreadful news to bring to Fräulein Adler."

One or two more questions established that the governess had no more to offer, and she was dismissed.

Holmes turned to Irene Adler.

"When you learned of this, did you inform the police?" said he.

"I was on the point of doing so, when—"

She made as if to rise, and I frowned at her. With the strain she had been undergoing, the less activity the better.

"When what?" asked Holmes.

"This telegram was delivered to me."

"What telegram?" Holmes inquired in a near-shout.

Miss Adler pushed herself up from the sofa and walked to the writing-desk.

"I am about to show it to you, Sherlock. Try not to be so impatient."

"I ask your pardon," said Holmes. "When a problem absorbs me, I tend to neglect the formalities."

A hint of dryness revealed itself in Irene Adler's voice as she said, "The problem absorbs me, too."

She removed a buff-colored sheet of paper from the desk and handed it to him.

Holmes read the telegram aloud in a rapid mutter: " 'Do nothing, stop. Tell no one, stop. Further instructions will be forthcoming, stop. Disobey these orders and you face the direst consequences—' "

"Stop!" cried Irene Adler, with ghastly appositeness.

She wavered where she stood, and I moved quickly to her side, supporting her with a hand under one elbow and another on her back.

"Here, now!" I said. "Sit back down. Have some more brandy."

Walking unsteadily, she allowed me to guide her to

the sofa and sank back on to its cushioned softness.

"I'm sorry," said she. "I thought I was stronger."

I added a small amount of brandy to her glass.

Her face, normally alert and vivacious, with a quality that could convey an impression of supreme vitality to the last row of a theater, now bore a pinched, drawn look. She gave a deep sigh, and spoke in a low, almost resigned tone.

"There it is, Sherlock. I have been waiting, waiting, *waiting* for those 'further instructions' since four o'clock this afternoon!" She glanced at the clock on the mantelshelf. "And it is now nearly nine-thirty! *What has happened to my son?*"

The peal of the front-door bell came as if in answer to her cry. She gave a gasp of fear and half rose from the sofa.

"It's the message!" she cried.

I sprang to the window, flung aside the curtain, and stepped on to the balcony. I saw below me a carriage and its driver, and, almost directly beneath my feet, a foreshortened form on the steps of the house. Running back into the drawing-room, I flung a quick report over my shoulder as I headed for the archway leading to the stairs.

"Closed carriage, Holmes—one horse—man at the reins—another at the door!"

A shouted "Wait!" from Holmes brought me to a momentary halt. He dashed past me and down the stairs. I paused at the top landing, and was aware that Irene Adler had come up behind me.

I could see Heller in the doorway, just turning to look at the fast-approaching Sherlock Holmes. The butler was holding in his hand an envelope apparently just received from the man who had rung the doorbell. Holmes brushed past him, and the sound of his shoes clattering on the front steps mingled with the rumble of a departing carriage and the swift tap of shod hooves on the cobbles.

In a moment he re-entered the hallway, his face dark with anger. Evidently, like Frau Reichenbach, he had been unable to gain any useful information from his brief view of the carriage. His gaze fell upon Heller, and, with an uncharacteristic show of temper, he vented his ire upon the unfortunate man.

"What are you standing there for? What is it? Deliver the letter to your mistress at once!"

"But, sir," the butler said in an injured tone, "it's not addressed to Miss Adler."

"Not? Not addressed to her? To whom is it addressed, then?"

Heller held out the envelope.

"To you, sir."

"What? What? Here, hand it over, then!"

Holmes ripped it open savagely and snatched out a sheet of heavy notepaper. As he read it, he stiffened, and the febrile irritation that had animated his actions and speech for the last few moments seemed to fall away from him. When he looked up to the head of the stairs where Irene Adler and I stood, his face was grave.

After a moment, he spoke, and there was a world of weariness in his voice.

"I had better read this to you." He glanced down at the note again. " 'The life of Scott Adler depends upon one thing alone, Mr. Sherlock Holmes, your refusal to cooperate with the police. You will refuse, and you will give no reason for your refusal or . . . the boy . . . will die.' "

Holmes had managed to finished reading the note aloud only with difficulty, and seemed to dread looking once more at Irene Adler.

By the time he raised his eyes, he did not have to be concerned about meeting her gaze: upon hearing the contents of the letter, she had turned perfectly white, and then fainted in my arms.

"Holmes!" I bellowed; and he rushed to help me support her.

Together we carried her to the sofa and set her down in as comfortable a position as possible. Though she was pale, and her pulse was both light and rapid, she seemed to be in no real trouble, and in fact might take some benefit from her short period of unconsciousness. My greatest fear, in fact, was that, once recovered, her concern and agitation—bound to be increased by the contents of the letter—would prevent her from sleeping at all, thus putting a dangerous strain on her nervous system.

I took one of my cards from my note-case, scribbled on it the ingredients of a mild sleeping-draught, and handed it to Heller.

"Here, take this round to the nearest chemist's, and—"

"A chemist, sir? Do you mean a scientist? I don't—"

"A pharmacy, man! A drugstore," said Holmes impatiently.

"Oh, yes, sir. There's one on Fourth Avenue."

"Whatever you call the place, give the man there this card. I doubt you'll need a prescription; he's probably got the powders made up under some trade name I'm not familiar with. Be off with you, now!"

Though Irene Adler was stirring fretfully by the time Heller returned, a packet of the powders dissolved in water allowed her to sink into a calm drowsiness which, by the time we left, had not yet deepened into sleep.

"If she's still awake in an hour's time," said I as we took our leave of Heller on the front steps, "see that she takes another packet of those powders."

The butler gave a slight bow.

"Yes, sir. Thank you, sir. Good night, gentlemen," he said.

He closed the door, and Holmes and I made our way down the steps to the street that fronted on the small park.

"That ought to take care of matters until morning, Holmes," said I. "Shall we look for a cab? We ought to be able to find one on the next street over, I should say."

"I should prefer to walk," said Sherlock Holmes in a colorless tone.

I looked up and saw from a sign at a street corner that we were at Twenty-first Street. I subtracted that number from forty-four, the number of the street that our hotel was in, and quickly enough saw that we had some twenty-three streets to traverse in a northward direction, plus one or more avenues to the west. I had no notion, however, how far apart the streets were, so was unable to estimate what sort of distance Holmes' projected walk involved. It was a mild night, though, and, after the stuffiness of the closed house and the atmosphere of fear and depression that pervaded it, I was glad of the fresh air and exercise.

"Whatever you say," said I cheerfully.

As we walked along, eventually turning to the north on an avenue which, curiously enough, bore the name of one Madison rather than a number, I looked about me with interest. The area, with its shops and blocks of flats and offices, was not unlike certain parts of London, say the eastern end of Oxford Street, yet the shapes of the buildings and their uniform modernity never failed to make it clear that we were in a foreign land.

I had hoped that the walk might enliven Holmes' wits and encourage him to discuss with me his notions of the problems we faced, but he seemed sunk in morose introspection, and strode heavily along with bowed head, taking no notice of his surroundings. At length, when the mounting value of the street numbers told me we were not far from the Algonquin Hotel, I ventured to speak.

"Can you make head or tail of it at all, Holmes? *I* can't."

In the same dead voice with which he had last spoken, Sherlock Holmes answered, "I am being manipulated."

"Eh? What's that? Manipulated? How d'you mean?"

"The chink in my armor, Watson. That weakness,

unknown to me, which Moriarty *must* have had in mind in making his threat. It's been discovered."

This sort of morbid vaporing was quite unlike Holmes, and I did not like the sound of it.

As heartily as I could, I said, "I'm sure I haven't the slightest notion of what you're talking about."

Sherlock Holmes looked at me for a moment, then continued his walk in silence. I was gazing with some interest at a shop-window display of a profusion of gramophones far greater than that available in England, several placarded with claims of the highest fidelity of reproduction, and marvelling at the inventive genius that had made it possible for the voices of the famous—and, to a limited extent, the music of the age—to be preserved for future centuries, when next he spoke. His remark, prompted by I knew not what vagaries of his roving mind, was of an almost alarming inconsequence.

"Do you know my full name, Watson?"

"Why, I don't believe I do."

I forbore to ask the reason for his question, being briefly seized with the dismal idea that he had a premonition of sudden death and wished me to have the information for his death certificate. I firmly rid myself of this dreary notion and resolved not to be infected by Holmes' sepulchral manner.

"It is William Scott Sherlock Holmes," he told me.

It was difficult to know what response to make to this. I might have answered in kind by telling him that my own second name was Hamish, except that he was already aware of that. But some sort of comment seemed to be called for.

"Is it, now? No, I didn't know that. William for the Conqueror, eh, and Scott for Sir Walter, I dare say. I wonder if that's where Irene Adler—" I still did not feel comfortable in using "Miss" in connection with any reference to her son—"picked up her lad's name; I expect his works are popular on the Continent." I was quite aware that this was sheer nervous drivelling, and resolved to change the subject to something more nearly approaching our concerns. "I say, Holmes, there *is* one thing that puzzles me."

A reluctant smile brightened my friend's saturnine countenance. *"One* thing? I commend your clarity of mind, Watson. What one thing is that?"

"That bit in the letter about not cooperating with the police. Why, Holmes, nobody's *asked* you to cooperate with the police!"

We were now in Forty-fourth Street, only a few yards from the hotel. The warm light from its lobby spilled on to the pavement, and, at the edge of the patch of illumination, I observed two men standing, as if in wait. I stopped Holmes with an urgent hand on his arm, and indicated the pair.

"Could they be watchers—or worse—sent by Moriarty?" said I in a voice not pitched to carry to them.

Holmes cocked his head and studied the two men for a moment, then murmured, "I fancy not, Watson. One, at least, has another look entirely."

He strode boldly toward the hotel, though his face was tight, with the expression of a man bracing himself for an ordeal he must endure.

The taller and younger of the two men, seemingly about the detective's own age, stepped forward. He was dressed plainly but neatly, and his voice, though not cultured, was firm.

"Mr. Sherlock Holmes?" he asked.

"Yes—my name's Holmes."

My friend stopped, and I with him.

The man who had accosted us doffed his bowler. "Inspector Lafferty. New York City Police Department."

I looked at Holmes. Moments ago, I had pointed out that the police had not asked his aid in any matter, and now here was a policeman, almost certainly on the point of requesting just such aid. If the letter spoke truth, for Sherlock Holmes to grant that request would be to sign Scott Adler's death-warrant!

Chapter Eight

The man with the Inspector, a portly chap of perhaps sixty, dressed in a light topcoat with a velvet collar, stepped forward in turn.

"And I'm Mortimer McGraw, President of the International Gold Exchange,". he announced.

I had a sudden sensation that we were being watched, and glanced around sharply. Then, in spite of the tension of the situation, I felt half inclined to laugh. There was indeed an eye focussed upon us, but it was a huge painted one staring from a signboard, one of a pair hanging from the shoulders of one of those men employed to trudge the streets as walking hoardings, advertising various businesses. The legend around the staring orb proclaimed that one McVay, proprietor of a chop-house, had "his Eye on YOU!" As the sandwich-man, clad in a cheap but colorful checked suit, ambled by, I observed that his rearward sign was also anatomical in theme, with a crudely limned giant finger pointing at the beholder, and the printed statement that this same McVay "means YOU!" I could well imagine that that unwinking stare might induce the fainter-hearted to give their patronage to the chop-house mentioned.

Holmes gave the grotesque ambulatory advertisement a passing glance, and was evidently not inclined to be amused by it.

He said, indicating me, "Dr. Watson," and I murmured, "Inspector. Mr. McGraw."

"Mr. Holmes," said Lafferty earnestly, "I only just

now found out you were in the city, or I'd have come to see you earlier."

"Oh? About what would that be?"

Lafferty gazed about him at the still-thronged street, and indicated a closed carriage standing by the curb.

"Mr. McGraw," he explained, "has been kind enough to give us the lend of his landau. Could we trouble you—both of you—to join us for a short drive?"

I darted a suspicious glance at the vehicle, but was able to assure myself that it in no wise resembled the style of the one which I had seen outside Irene Adler's house. After all, anyone could *say* that he was an inspector of police . . . but Holmes was not the man to be taken in by any such imposture.

All the same, my friend hesitated a moment before saying, "As you wish."

"Thank you, Mr. Holmes," said McGraw quietly but fervently. "All right!" he called to the landau's driver as we crossed the pavement and clambered in.

Holmes and I were urged to take the forward-facing seat, with the Inspector and Mr. McGraw opposite us.

After we had moved slowly along the street—so much more brightly lit than most of our London thoroughfares!—for a few moments with no one speaking, Holmes pulled out his watch and consulted it.

"Well, gentlemen?" said he. "It's almost eleven at night. Had we not better get to the meat of this?"

McGraw leaned forward.

"Mr. Holmes," he inquired, "have you ever heard of the International Gold Exchange?"

"I am sure you are prepared to correct that deficiency in my knowledge on the spot, sir."

Holmes spoke so flatly as to appear almost hostile, and I sensed that the other two men were beginning to be somewhat puzzled. Knowing what I did of what had occurred that evening, and the dire contents of the note now folded in the pocket of his tailcoat, I could understand, as they could not, the conflict that raged within him and found expression in his indifferent tone.

"Gold is a very attractive metal to thieves, as you well know," McGraw continued. "It is also the major medium of exchange between the nations of the civilized world."

"Quite."

"Shipment of large quantities of gold from one country to another is not only arduous but dangerous. Because of that fact, the International Gold Exchange was established. May I describe it for you?"

I own that my ears pricked up at this. I am no more greedy than the next man, but gold, whether in the form of the legends of Golconda and the 'Forty-niners, or a sovereign piece to clink in one's pocket, has always fascinated me. Had I become a dentist, I suppose I should have come to regard it as merely another material of my profession, though that is by the way.

Holmes, in any case, did not share my interest, but merely replied, "Of course."

McGraw warmed to his account as it progressed.

"Deep beneath the basement of the Bouwerie National Bank here in Manhattan," he said, "cut into the bedrock of the island, are a number of vaults, each considered the property of the sovereign nation whose name appears above its steel door. In each vault is stored almost *all* of that nation's gold reserve. At the last official count, over two hundred billion dollars' worth of bullion occupied these vaults."

I was slightly nonplussed, the term "billion" being unfamiliar to me. I supposed it to be some multiple of a million, perhaps an American term for our familiar "milliard." If so—or even, for that matter, if not— Mr. McGraw was talking of a very considerable sum indeed.

"I see," said Sherlock Holmes. "I think I understand the object of your exchange, Mr. McGraw. Correct any inaccuracies on my part, if you will. When gold is to be transferred from one country—Russia, let us say—to another—as it might be, England—instead of making the long and hazardous journey from St.

Petersburg to London, the required amount of gold bullion is merely removed from one vault and placed in the appropriate one near it."

"Exactly! Six trusted employees of the Exchange now do the work that used to take six *hundred* subjects of the countries involved, and the risk of theft has been reduced to virtually nothing!"

"Most ingenious," commented Holmes. "I congratulate you. I have only one question to ask."

"And that is?" McGraw said, as Holmes gave him a cool look.

"Why am I being told this at this hour of the night and under this notable precaution of secrecy?"

Lafferty drummed his fingers on the bowler he held in his lap, and let out a long sigh, as if reluctant to say what he must. Then he got to his point with a rush.

"Because the gold's been stolen, that's why!"

Holmes leaned forward, keen and alert for the first time since the note had been delivered to him. It was impossible for such a man as he not to take an interest in so massive a crime, no matter what threats had been made to prevent him involving himself with the police.

"*All of it?*" he inquired in excitement—I might almost have written "delight."

"All but two bricks or so," McGraw answered morosely.

"Great heavens, how?" said I.

"We haven't the slightest idea." Lafferty's tone was sour in the extreme.

"When was the theft discovered?" said Sherlock Holmes.

"Four days ago, during a routine inspection of the vaults. When we unlocked the door at the bottom of the elevator shaft, the vaults were empty!" McGraw explained.

"And," the Inspector added, "there was a huge hole cut into the rear wall of the chamber!"

"A hole leading where?"

"Into the subway excavation that goes right past the bank! We found one brick of bullion in the tunnel, another in the excavation."

"And news of this incredible theft has been kept from the public?" Holmes asked.

McGraw answered this question.

"So far. But, Mr. Holmes, in forty-eight hours' time a transaction is due to take place between Italy and Germany. When that happens, the theft will be discovered, and the international repercussions will be such that not even war—world-wide war!—can be ruled out!"

I shuddered. A newspaper I had been able to glance at that very afternoon during a rest I gave myself from unpacking had carried a dispatch from Berlin concerning a hysterical diatribe the Emperor had delivered to his troops, demanding their protection from a revolt that appeared to exist only in his mind. With so unstable a personality occupying the throne of one of the great Powers—and the rulers of many of the others, for that matter, not being notable for good sense—the catastrophe Mr. McGraw envisaged did not seem as implausible as I should have liked.

The Inspector now spoke with great urgency.

"Mr. Holmes, we've got forty-eight hours to find that gold and get it back to its vaults with no one the wiser—and we need *your* help to do it!"

Mr. McGraw chimed in, "Mr. Holmes, the fate of the world may well hang in the balance!"

I joined the other two in staring intently at Sherlock Holmes, though there was this difference: they were looking for the first signs of an assent they took for granted, whilst I steeled myself to watch the torment that racked that proud face as he prepared to say what, only hours ago, both he and I would have considered unthinkable. A slight movement of his arm told me that his hand was even now clenched around the note that deprived him of his liberty of action as much as its writer had deprived Scott Adler of his.

The carriage slowed, and I realized that our course

had taken us back to the hotel. As it stopped, Holmes, appearing older and wearier than I had ever seen him, looked from one to the other of the two men facing him.

"I am sorry, gentlemen. But I am unable to assist you in this matter."

He began to rise from his seat, and reached for the door-handle.

"You *what!*" Lafferty's voice was a yelp of outrage.

"I can be of no service to you whatsoever."

Holmes opened the door and stepped from the carriage. I scrambled after him and stood beside him on the pavement.

Inspector Lafferty leaned from the coach and said, his voice mingling incredulity with scorn, "Have I been talking to Sherlock Holmes?"

"You have been. I now must ask you to permit me to bid you a good evening."

He bowed to the men in the carriage, turned, and made for the hotel. He was forced to wait for an instant as the sandwich-man with the puffery for the philocular chop-house proprietor I had observed earlier passed by on yet another lap of his nightly rounds. Before Holmes and I could gain the shelter of the lobby, a bellow from Lafferty halted us.

"Wait a minute! You can't just turn us down like this! We've come to you because of your world-wide reputation! Mr. McGraw's explained the seriousness of the—"

With an icy manner that told me of the pain he was concealing, Holmes turned and said, "I'm afraid I have nothing further to say to you."

Lafferty was now leaning out of the carriage, carried away by honest rage.

"Well, I've got something to say to you, Mister!"

"Inspector!" McGraw's voice was hoarse with embarrassment, and he plucked futilely at the policeman's sleeve.

"When the crime's found out, and it's learned it could lead to a world war—"

"Inspector, please! Shh!"

"—and Sherlock Holmes knew about it and wouldn't lift a finger to assist the police . . . what's everyone going to think—"

McGraw, clearly agonized both at the noisy scene being made and the thought of what passers-by might guess at from it, called quickly up to his coachman, "Drive on!"

The vehicle started with a jerk that dumped Lafferty back into his seat but did not stay his tirade.

"—of Sherlock Holmes *then?*"

That was the last we heard of him as the carriage trundled off and was lost to view. I did not dare to look at Holmes' face in that moment. I had seen him tried sorely, but never humiliated to his face without the possibility of defending himself. As I followed him up the broad flight of marble stairs off the lobby to our room, I found myself fuming at the Inspector's savage attack.

"The scoundrel!" I muttered. "How dare he?"

Holmes' voice was soft and emotionless. "Now do you understand what I meant when I spoke of being manipulated? *Now* do you fully appreciate the art, the genius, of this Napolean of crime?"

"What Napoleon are you talking about?" I fear that my mind was battered by the succession of bombshells exploded against it that evening, and for a moment the meaning of my friend's not very difficult metaphor eluded me. "Oh! Well, he's had his Austerlitz and Marengo, but I dare say Moscow and Waterloo are—"

Holmes slapped his right fist in the open palm of his left hand.

"He *knew* those mutilated tickets would bring me to New York—and contrived, by the Devil's luck or shrewd intelligence work, to travel on the very same ship! He *knew* I would be at the theater tonight, and that the announcement of Irene Adler's 'indisposition' would make me rush to her home, so that he could deliver that note to me!"

Outside our room, numbered 215, although it was on the first story above the lobby—Americans, I believe, count the ground floors of their buildings as the first, which makes little sense—Holmes drew a key from his pocket and inserted it in the lock. Before turning it, he addressed me yet again.

"He *knew* that Inspector Lafferty would be waiting for me here at the hotel, would enlist my aid in the recovery of the gold—and that, because of Scott Adler, I would be forced to refuse to offer it."

Inside the room, after having tossed aside his hat and shrugged out of his opera cloak, he sank dejectedly into a chair and continued his monologue.

"Every single thing Moriarty promised that night in London has come true! The crime of the century *has* been committed. And I *am* helpless to do anything about it!"

I carefully folded my cloak and placed it in the wardrobe, draped the tailcoat over a chair, as the hotel valet would need to sponge and press it in the morning, undid my carefully knotted tie, and let out a sigh of relaxation as I removed my front collar stud, allowing the collar's two crimped ends to spring apart like the tips of an unstrung bow and the two halves of my starched shirt bosom to part company. I had been too keyed up to be aware of it, but full evening dress is not the most comfortable of uniforms for such activity as Holmes and I had undertaken that night.

"Then you think," said I, "that Moriarty made off with all that gold?"

"And with Scott Adler, I'm convinced of it!"

I was willing to credit the Professor with the will to undertake any kind of villainy, but was not yet convinced of all points in this case. For one thing, moving that amount of gold seemed to me more a job for a firm of carters than for a master criminal; for another...

"What the deuce can he *do* with all that bullion?" I asked Holmes.

"You heard McGraw. He can bring the nations of

the world to the brink of a war that would engulf the planet."

"Well, but what good's a world war to Moriarty?"

"None to him, or anyone, of course—it's the *prevention* of it! With mankind poised over the abyss of unimaginable devastation, Professor Moriarty will come forward, reveal that the gold is in his possession, and that the world's bankrupt nations are in his power! Moriarty, ruler of the world! The crime of all centuries to come? Indeed it is, Watson, indeed it is! And I?"

Eyes glaring like those of a trapped eagle, he snatched the note from his pocket and held it up in a clenched hand. Its pallid hue seemed to infuse the air with the menace of Professor Moriarty's evil presence.

Holmes' voice was almost cracking with fury and self-contempt as he cried, "I am powerless to circumvent it!"

He crumpled the note and dashed it to the floor, then rushed from the sitting-room into the bedroom.

I stooped to retrieve the wad of paper, smoothed it, and placed it on a table. It was evidence, after all, and it made no sense to destroy it. I sighed, grieved at my friend's trouble—and concerned for the dreadful repercussions that Moriarty's audacious enterprise might bring about—and set to work on removing the last of the studs from my shirt. I have always, in taking studs from a dress-shirt, tried to leave the stiffly starched surface unmarred; a legacy, I suppose, from my student days, when laundry charges loomed very large in a limited budget, and a stiff-bosomed shirt spared for a second wearing meant a distinct savings. That is not a consideration now, but I take a modest pride in maintaining my skill. I was, therefore, somewhat vexed when a discordant noise from the bedroom startled me as I was easing the stud out, and caused me to wrench it loose, crumpling and distorting the stiffened fabric around the button-hole.

Sherlock Holmes was at his blessed violin again,

not drawing from it the gay, smooth sounds that had enlivened the ship's concert, but those harsh scrapings, growlings, whines, and eerie drones that he made it produce when improvising to fit his mood. As always, something in the sound jangled deep in my being, making me first uneasy, then distinctly edgy, and finally positively short-tempered.

I rose and passed by the open bedroom door, clearing my throat ostentatiously, in the hope that Holmes would take the hint and desist. He paid no attention, and the noise continued. He was hunched over the instrument, sawing away with an abstracted glare in his eyes, and a flood of impatience with the whole business—Moriarty, Irene Adler, the wretched bricks of gold, Holmes' moods—welled up in me.

I stood in the bedroom doorway and said sternly, "Holmes!"

He looked up, his eyebrows raised in an expression of surprise, said, "Yes?"—and, thank goodness, ceased playing.

"Forgive me for saying so, Holmes," I ventured, letting the words come in a rush, "but if you're prepared to—to sit there and . . . *fiddle* while the world goes up in smoke, well, then, your precious Professor Moriarty *deserves* to sit on his mountain of gold and—and—tell the rest of us to go jump!"

I was aware, as I strode away from the bedroom, that I had not been totally coherent or reasoned, but at least I had, for once, let Mr. Sherlock Holmes know pretty clearly how I felt! However, when I heard him enter the sitting-room behind me, and turned to face him, I confess that I felt rather abashed at my show of pique.

Holmes, holding his violin and bow loosely, looked at me with what appeared to be respectful interest. If he was, perhaps, amused at my outburst, at least he no longer wore the tragic expression that had been his for so many hours.

"Well," said I. "Well . . . I've never made any bones about what that infernal fiddle does to my nerves!"

"It's quite all right," said Sherlock Holmes. "You've no need to apologize, Watson. Indeed, it is I— Hello!"

He had stiffened, and was looking out the window that gave on to the street, nostrils flared and eyes ablaze, his whole form possessing that eager tension which resembles that of a hunting dog at the point.

"What . . . have . . . we . . . here?" he enunciated slowly.

I crossed to stand beside him, my long experience with him and his work prompting me to stand to one side of the window, and peered into the street. On the opposite side, the sandwich-man for the chop-house whom I had taken note of twice during the evening was leaning against a wall. Though he was at some distance, the lurid eye on the sign was unmistakable.

"What is it, Holmes?" I asked.

"That man down there is watching this room. I saw him twice this evening, marching up and down with his signboards."

"I saw him, too. But—watching us, is he? I wonder what he's up to?"

"I can tell you that, Watson!" cried Holmes, an almost feverish touch of color staining his pale cheeks. "He's wondering what *we're* up to!" He turned away from the window. "My dear friend, I owe you a profound debt of gratitude!"

"Come now, Holmes," said I, feeling quite ill at ease.

"I do, Watson, I do! Had you not reprimanded me as you did, I should have gone on doing exactly what you accused me of doing: fiddling while the world burned! Moriarty would, indeed, have won the day. But you broke the spell, my friend, and washed my mind clear as a sparkling brook!"

He was truly out of the dumps now, pacing the room from end to end, fairly crackling with energy and enthusiasm.

"*Why* are we being watched, Watson? Ask yourself that question!"

"Well, there's no need to. You just asked it."

"And I'll answer it. If Moriarty's plan is so perfect—if I am thought to be helpless, destroyed, unable to fight him—as indeed I thought myself until a moment ago—then *why is it necessary to have me watched?*"

There was triumph, not inquiry, in his voice as he flung out the sentence like a challenge—a challenge to mortal struggle offered to someone not present in that room.

Chapter Nine

Though I was beginning to see the direction of Sherlock Holmes' reasoning, I was reluctant to make the same leap to a conclusion.

"Holmes, that's not an answer. It's another question," said I.

"And the answer is: because the plan's not perfect! It has got one single flaw in it, and that man down there has to be there so Moriarty will know at once if I've discovered that flaw!"

"Well, and have you?"

Holmes looked almost gleeful.

"Yes, but he's not going to find that out! Watson, what is it that prevents my assisting the police?"

"Why, the lad's safety, of course."

"Of course! So long as Scott Adler remains Moriarty's captive, my hands are tied! His life hangs upon my inactivity. But, Watson—what if the lad were snatched from Moriarty's claws, and set free?"

It was clear that that would indeed alter matters, but raised a pertinent question, which I put.

"By whom?"

"By *us!* And in such a way that Moriarty still thinks him held prisoner! If that can be achieved, the manacles fall from my wrists and I am free to turn my attention to the theft of the gold!"

I gave a doubtful grunt.

"Easier said than done, I should say."

Holmes' dry manner was precisely that of his old self now.

"Yes, Watson, it's what you *would* say, and indeed what you *have* said."

He turned and went into the bedroom again, and I wandered over to the window for another cautious look at our watcher. In most circumstances, such a spy would be cause for alarm, but so turned-about was this case that his sinister pretence was in fact the first sign of hope!

I observed him for a moment, and called to the next room, "Chap's still out there. Damp night, too—the pavement's getting slick. He'll have a nice touch of rheumatism by morning, and I wish him joy of it! Holmes, you're not going to start up on that wretched fiddle again, are you—? Oh!"

For I turned to see Sherlock Holmes coming into the sitting-room clad in his purple dressing-gown, holding his massive pipe and the bulging tobacco pouch he carried with him on his journeys, the knife-transfixed Persian slipper which usually served that purpose being traditionally unremovable from Baker Street and, in any case, not practical for travelling.

"We're in for one of those sessions, are we?" said I.

"Precisely."

Holmes gathered a number of cushions from the chairs in the sitting-room and placed them in a pile on the sofa. Seating himself cross-legged on this heap, he opened the pouch and poured out a conical pile of tobacco on to the low table in front of him, then set about methodically tamping pinches of it into the bowl of the pipe.

"Don't let me detain you, Watson," he said. "I expect this is a four-pipe problem, at the very least."

The pipe filled to his satisfaction, he struck a match on the polished surface of the table, leaving a scar—I calculated that would add a shilling or so, or "bits" as I believe the local term is, to our bill at the end or our stay—and sucked the flame hungrily down into the packed tobacco. As the first smoke trickled into his mouth, his face assumed the tranquil, immobile look of one in a trance, a look which, I knew of old, signalled absolute concentration on the matter at hand.

"Yes, well . . . take care you don't set the upholstery afire the way you did that night in Ashby-de-la-Zouche," I cautioned him.

I knew full well that he did not hear me; nor did I much care. To see Holmes himself again, and bringing the diamond-sharp point of that great intellect to bear on the problem before us, was worth any amount of scorch marks on the Algonquin's furniture.

Pausing at the bedroom door, I looked back at Holmes, already wreathed in a nimbus of blue smoke. He bore a not undignified resemblance to the Caterpillar, perched on his mushroom and puffing away at his hookah, portrayed in the illustrations to *Alice's Adventures in Wonderland*.

"Good night, Holmes."

There was no reply, so I provided one.

" 'Night, Watson. Sleep well," said I to myself.

Apparently I took this injunction literally, for I was asleep the moment my head hit the pillow, and awoke, feeling refreshed—although with a slight soreness in my feet as a result of our long trek the night before, and the twinge in the leg with which my legacy from the Battle of Maiwand reminded me of its accuracy as a herald of damp weather. The well-rested feeling was tainted with a slight sensation of alarm, as though some danger portended, such as fire. I glanced at the open transom over the bedroom door. Of course!

Wrapping my dressing-gown about me, and noting that the cord that held it at the waist seemed to be shrinking slowly (probably a characteristic of the cheap Egyptian cotton now flooding the English market), I entered the sitting-room. Except that the prevailing tone was blue-gray rather than yellow, I might almost have been walking into a London pea-souper. The stale smoke that filled the room stung my eyes and throat, and, until I became accustomed to it, made Holmes' seated form—unchanged, as far as I could tell, from the position in which I had last seen it—difficult to discern. No wonder I had awakened to a feeling that something was burning!

"Phew!" I exclaimed. "I'm surprised nobody's called the fire brigade."

I went to the window and opened it, savoring the damp morning air, and at the same time observing, though careful to appear to be looking in another direction, the post where last night's watcher had stood.

"Hello! Chap's been replaced, Holmes. This one's wearing stripes, not checks." With the air a little clearer, I turned back to the room, and noticed that the heap of tobacco on the table had been reduced to a few scattered crumbs. "Well, Holmes, what have you come up with?"

Though he had clearly not slept at all, and looked quite drawn about the cheekbones, he was as alert as I have ever known him, and said briskly, "Two points of interest, Watson, about which I shall be delighted to enlighten you while you're dressing."

It was actually while I was shaving that Holmes expounded his first "point of interest," and, had I not been steeled to surprises from my friend, I might well have given myself a veritable Heidelberg dueling scar with the keen blade.

"Scott Adler's abductor was a woman."

I hastily withdrew the razor from my throat and looked at it. There were only shaving soap and whisker-ends on the cutting edge; no tinge of red.

"But that's impossible!" I said.

"The conclusion is inescapable."

I returned to my task, and Holmes to his expounding.

"How did Frau Reichenbach's assailant begin the assault?" he asked.

"Grabbed her by the hair," said I.

"The instinctive target of a *woman* when she finds herself in combat with another of her own gender. And what did the good lady's assailant do then?"

"Kicked her," answered I, as clearly as I could,

considering that I was engaged in that tricky part of the shave where one has to stretch the upper lip very tightly in order to get at the corners of the mouth.

In the event, Holmes appeared to understand me well enough.

"In the shins," he said. "Another instinctive form of female attack!"

I washed the shaving soap from my face and went into the bedroom in search of the shirt and tie I had laid out.

"I must say, Holmes, none of the ladies *I've* had anything to do with—"

"I never mentioned ladies, Watson, I merely said a woman. *And* one of sufficient strength to fling Frau Reichenbach to the ground, seize young Scott Adler—"

Part of my mind was aware that the brown-and-gray tie I was putting on seemed rather drab in this vivid city, and I was speculating about whether I might have time to visit one or two New York shops. The main portion was objecting to Holmes' proposition.

"Holmes, now you're assuming too much! It's all very well to say a woman struck that governess and pummelled her in the manner you describe, but that's a far cry from seizing a nine-year-old boy who's struggling and crying out!"

Holmes' reply to this trenchant objection was an unrepentant "Aha!"

A knocking at the hallway door now summoned him to the sitting-room.

As he went, he turned and said, "Admirable, my dear Watson!—Come in, then, waiter!—You've hit upon the *second* point."

As I entered the sitting-room, a hotel waiter was pushing in a rolling cart covered with a profusion of covered dishes.

"Eh? I have?" said I. "What is it, then?"

Holmes lifted the metal covers from some of the dishes and sniffed at them appreciatively. From one there arose a tempting aroma of egg, though what was visible was a strange yellow mass, all scrambled together.

"No mention," Holmes went on, making an emphatic gesture with a cover he held, "was made by Frau Reichenbach of *any* struggling or outcry. Thank you."

This last was to the waiter, and accompanied by a passed coin which drew a pleased response.

Holmes began laying out the dishes on the low table in front of the sofa, while I restored the piled cushions in its center to their rightful places.

"By George, you're right," I said.

"So it must be assumed none was made."

Holmes turned some of the strangely treated eggs on to a plate, surrounded the heap with several slices of bacon, a nicely browned piece of ham, and some sausages. As I lifted some of the covers, looking in vain for a grilled tomato or a hearty piece of smoked herring—even a devilled kidney, though these were not my favorites—I made the next leap in logic.

"A lad being seized suddenly must *inevitably* cry out, Holmes. Therefore, the report itself is false, and Frau Reichenbach is implicated!"

"Pretty, very pretty, Watson, but I fancy it won't hold water. I am convinced that our governess' account is correct, and that the strange business of the boy who raised no outcry is akin to the affair of the dog that did nothing in the night-time, which you have been good enough to preserve in your writings."

"The dog did not bark . . ." I recalled.

"Because it knew the intruder."

"And the boy . . ."

"Was party to the arrangement! I'm convinced, Watson, that the lad knew of all this in advance."

I started upright in my chair and laid down my fork.

"What! Scott Adler co-operate with Moriarty in his own kidnapping? Now, Holmes!"

"Suppose," said Sherlock Holmes, "that it were put to him as a joke of sorts?"

This seemed to me the sort of explanation which clears up one point only at the cost of bringing up another as difficult.

"A joke on whom? Surely not on his mother?"

"Perhaps on Frau Reichenbach."

I considered this, taking a sip of the hotel's excellent coffee (I had regretted the absence of tea, but then decided that, in this country, tea would probably be a travesty in any case), and finally nodded. I could see that a spirited boy, condemned to be escorted through New York's exciting streets by that starched Teuton, might well come to regard her as a suitable butt for a prank. That part of it was all very well, then, but ...

"Yes, but for what *reason?*" I asked Holmes. "And why a woman kidnapper in the first place?"

"Because the boy must be kept somewhere," said Holmes, "quietly and inconspicuously, and what better place could there be than a respectable lodging-house, and what better guardian than someone who might be taken for his cousin, his aunt, even his mother? There's our salvation, Watson! Had he been spirited away to some criminal den in this teeming city about which we know so little we should have been at a standstill. In time, neighborhood gossip—for eyes are as sharp in New York's slums as in London's, I'll be bound—might have brought the matter to police attention, but far too late to do us any good.

"But take those two curious points about the abduction, and all else falls into place! Given the woman kidnapper and the consenting victim, we know the circumstances in which he must be being held. It only remains to discover the actual address. And we know one more thing: where to set about finding that!"

"Where?"

Holmes had finished what he cared to of the breakfast provided us—though there were one or two things I still fancied—and rose from the table.

"At number four, Gramercy Park West. I have some questions I must put to Irene at once, Watson. Will that sedative you gave her have worn off by now?"

My watch showed it to be just short of eight—well past noon in London, I realized with a sudden surprise, for the first time aware of the immensity of the distance that separated us from our homeland.

I said, "I believe so."

"Excellent."

Holmes rummaged in the wardrobe and flung on a chair my waterproof coat and a sturdy hat, and his own Inverness and deerstalker cap. I left the table and joined him, eyeing with a certain regret an untasted heap of thin rounds of cooked dough, not unlike the *chupatties* of India, evidently meant to be garnished from a nearby pitcher of sweet brown liquid.

I eyed Holmes' fore-and-aft cap dubiously.

"Ought you not to wear something less distinctive, Holmes? With you in that rig, anyone keeping us under observation could do so from half a mile away."

Holmes settled the cap firmly on his head, saying, "If Professor Moriarty wishes to keep an eye on us, Watson, I see no need to be disobliging about it. You recall my little lecture to you on the *Pavonia* about disguising oneself impromptu?"

"Oh, yes. Altering one or two characteristic things so as to throw off a watcher's expectations."

"Precisely. It also works the other way."

He said no more on the point, and, trying to work out what he might mean, I followed him from the room.

The sedative powders had evidently done their work, for Irene Adler looked well-rested and far more composed than the night before, as she faced us on the sofa in her drawing-room. The window-curtains were looped back, and watery March sunshine flooded the room, making it seem altogether a more cheerful place—a room in which it might be possible to plan hopefully rather than, as had been the case less then twelve hours ago, endure scene after scene of shock and despair. The actress was clad in a pale-green négligée which, though perfectly modest, made me even more aware of the distance between London and New York than had the time difference.

"Irene," said Sherlock Holmes, "I want to know what you and Scott did the day before yesterday—*everything* you did."

She considered.

"Well, with *Mrs. Tanqueray* opening last night— I saw in the papers this morning that May Robson got good notices, by the way, and I'm glad for her—I've had a fairly constant rehearsal schedule for the last several days, and so wasn't able to spend as much time with Scott as I wished. So, when the tickets came, it was a good chance for an unexpected treat—"

"What tickets?"

"The Metropolitan Opera. The management sent round a complimentary pair of them. Scott's fond of *Aïda*, and has a tremendous crush on little Nicole Romaine—"

"And who is little Nicole Romaine?"

"Why, a member of the corps de ballet at the opera house," said Miss Adler.

Holmes snapped his fingers.

"Ah! Did you hear that, Watson? A *dancer*—and therefore by necessity strong, quick, agile, eh?" He turned once more to Irene Adler. "Is it usual for the management of the Metropolitan Opera to send you free tickets? Is it perhaps a customary courtesy to members of the theatrical profession?"

Her fair brow furrowed.

"Sometimes, if one has a friend in the company, it's possible to use a vacant seat, but . . . no, not sending tickets round to one's house. I don't recall that happening before."

"Could they then have been sent by someone *else?*"

Sherlock Holmes was evidently highly excited; Irene Adler, merely bewildered.

"Why, I simply never thought about it," she remarked.

"We must *now* think seriously about it! Tell me about Scott and this Nicole Romaine."

Irene Adler brightened.

"He's her pet. Whenever we go backstage after a performance—"

"Which you did on this occasion?"

"Yes."

"And they spoke together, these two, the little dancer and her pet?"

"Oh, my, yes. They were laughing and whispering in each other's ears for the longest time, like children in a schoolyard. She's scarcely more than a child herself."

Holmes rose from his chair and began pacing the room, as though the excitement rising in him demanded movement.

"*Whispering* in each other's ears. Did you hear that, Watson? And laughing! Hatching the plot right there, I've no doubt!"

"Plot? What plot? Do you tell me, Sherlock, that Scott—?"

"A plot, my dear Irene, in which you and your unfortunate son are leading players, working from a script you have not read but have yet followed to the very line! But now, though—now *I* shall assume a role in that plot, with some considerable departures from the script which I fancy our dramatist will not be pleased with!"

Holmes' pacing took him past the windows fronting the park, at which he abruptly stopped, directing a keen look out and downwards.

"Aha!" said he. "Our friend in the checkered suit is back."

I joined Holmes and saw the watcher of the night before, now lacking his advertising boards, leaning against the park railings opposite.

"Chap doesn't even have a change of clothes, it

seems," I observed. "Your precious Professor doesn't look after his troops very well, eh, Holmes?"

He ignored my comment and said in a musing tone, "It is vital that I leave this house unobserved..."

"I dare say there's a back way out."

Irene Adler nodded in confirmation of my guess.

"The same thought will have impressed itself upon Moriarty, and I have no doubt that he has provided for it. No. You and I, Watson, must appear to leave, thus drawing our friend out there away from here."

He crossed the room to where his Inverness and cap lay on a chair, picked them up, and returned to Irene Adler.

"I seem to recall," he said, "on a not-too-distant occasion, your remarkable impersonation of a young man." In spite of the gravity of the situation, the glance that passed between them held some amount of amusement, for it was that very impersonation that had signaled Holmes' defeat in their one encounter as antagonists. "Can you be equally deceptive in the guise of one... not so young as that?"

Irene Adler smiled up at him, then stood and reached for the cloak and cap.

"*I'm* not quite so young as that any more, Sherlock," said she.

In addition to her imposture, Miss Adler contributed a useful bit of stagecraft to our exit, suggesting that an air of confused urgency be created to excite and alarm our watcher, and blocking out the parts to be played by Holmes, myself, her butler, and herself.

Thus, the man in the checkered suit first saw Heller run outside and down the steps, bawling for a cab and waving his arms energetically; then saw the summoned vehicle, its driver infected with the butler's agitation, hasten to respond; then heard Sherlock Holmes, just inside the doorway, call impatiently, "Right along, Watson! *Right along!*"; then saw the unmistakable Inverness-and-deerstalker-clad figure of Holmes, with myself panting beside him, dash down the steps and into the cab, which immediately set off at a smart pace.

Peering through the back window of our carriage, I saw the watcher gesturing violently; and, just as we turned a corner and passed from his sight, a closed carriage drew up beside him, into which he bounded.

I relaxed and sat back next to Irene Adler. The plan was for us to go to the Algonquin, which she would enter, still in her character of Holmes, and leave a few moments later in her own. We would then, at intervals, make our separate ways back to her house and await the detective's report. I was not happy at being thus removed from the fray, yet I knew that this was one of those occasions on which my friend must be free to exercise his solitary genius in his own way. In any case, I was off duty for the moment, and might as well enjoy it.

I glanced at Irene Adler, recalling Dr. Johnson's comment about the bliss of riding in a post-chaise with a pretty woman. Well, Irene Adler was as pretty a woman as one could reasonably expect to encounter anywhere; and we were certainly riding, probably more comfortably than in a post-chaise of a century and more ago. Yet I wondered: how would Johnson have felt had his fair lady been wrapped from neck to ankle in an Inverness cape, half her face concealed by a deerstalker cap?

Once more I am removed from the stage to play my necessary but undemanding part, and must rely on later knowledge, mainly from his own account, to set down the doings of Mr. Sherlock Holmes for the remainder of that eventful day.

Chapter Ten

A smile of satisfaction crossed Sherlock Holmes' hawk-like face as he watched the man in the checkered suit spring into the carriage and set off after the departing cab. Moriarty's hounds would follow the scent laid for them to the Algonquin Hotel.

"And I," he murmured, "will be free to set the cat among his pigeons. Dear me! There's a mixed metaphor Watson would scarcely countenance."

Heller entered the drawing-room and reported that, as instructed, he had scanned the rear area-way, and had indeed observed someone lounging in a position which allowed him to oversee the back door to the house.

"Excellent, Heller! It is what I predicted, and therefore means that I have divined our adversary's plans correctly. Now, then, I want you to improvise a bit of stage business at the rear of the house: shaking out a dinner-cloth on the back steps, setting out the dustbins —I leave the details to you—so that our watcher's attention will be riveted upon you whilst I make my exit from the front door."

"I shall be glad to do it, sir," said Heller. "Though, strictly speaking, the tasks you describe are not my place. The kitchen maid—"

Holmes glared at him.

"Heller, I doubt that a hired thug is aware of the social distinctions that obtain below-stairs! This is a matter of great moment to your mistress, not one of housekeeping!"

"Of course, sir."

Heller bowed and left.

In a moment, Holmes let himself out the front door, and strolled casually to the north end of Gramercy Park and thence to the next street. As he walked, he sorted rapidly through his thoughts until they were arranged in an orderly sequence, and his next steps were clear in his mind. At one point, his meditations were interrupted by a frantic clangor, and he looked up to find himself in the middle of a major street, with an electric tramcar bearing down on him.

A broad-jump which would have done him credit during his Cambridge days took him to the opposite pavement, where a street loafer jeered at him: "Say, bo, was you waitin' fer de motorman t' send you a telegram dat he was comin' t'rough and would yiz be kind enough to git out o' de way? Dat stuff don't go, I'll tell you!"

Holmes looked at his mocker and snapped his fingers. The jibe had supplied the last—the obvious—missing element!

"Thank you, my good fellow," he said, and pressed a coin into the man's grimy paw.

"Chee," the loafer replied, looking at it with respect. "If I gets dat fer talkin' wise wid you, what's it wort' if I curses you out some?"

"One black eye, possibly two," answered Holmes, and strode up the street, mentally putting the finishing touches to his plan.

This was no more than the matter of a few moments, and, the task accomplished, he slowed his pace and allowed himself to become aware of his surroundings.

He was now at the edge of a large park surrounded by commercial buildings and hotels on three sides. One building, at the far edge, in what he took to be Fifth Avenue, rose dizzyingly high, and was built in a curious wedge shape, the sharp end pointing north—doubtless the aptly named Flatiron. The park was bordered to the east by a dazzling structure whose stone shone with a warm, golden hue. An impressive colonnade fronted on the park, and, above it, fanciful towers topped the building. This would be the famous Madison Square Garden, then. His gaze travelled upwards, and was caught by a glint of gold: the statue of a gracefully unadorned woman, poised on one toe, as if about to spring into the sky—Saint-Gaudens' Diana. She was the embodiment of the feminine and of the unreachable, and a muscle in Holmes' jaw twitched as he contemplated her. Unreachable . . . Whatever his successes, there was much that was, that always would be, unreachable. . . .

He shrugged away the brief reverie, and raised his hand to beckon to an approaching hansom.

Leaning on the scarred counter, Sherlock Holmes finished composing a message on the blank form, and passed it over to the manager of the office. The steady clatter of a battery of telegraph instruments in the rear filled the room, vying with the sounds of traffic on Broadway that came through the open door.

The manager scanned the message form and blinked at the address written on it.

"Excuse me, sir," said he, "but the opera house is just across the street. Wouldn't you rather—?"

"Thank you so much, but I prefer to have it delivered."

The manager scratched his head in perplexity, and said, "Well, yeah. But . . . I mean, we send telegrams by telegraph, don't you see—from one office to another, to the one that's nearest to the person you're sending it to. And *this* is already the nearest office to the Met. I don't see's we could send a telegram to ourselves, somehow."

Holmes said patiently, "Could you not merely have the message printed on one of your blanks, *without* sending it back and forth? I particularly want this to be received as a telegram—far more impressive to a lady than a note, don't you know?"

Holmes allowed one eye to droop meaningfully as he looked at the manager.

"Well, say, I guess we can do that," the man said.

"But I'll have to charge you the full rate, same's if it was sent from another office." He rapidly ran his pencil over the message, counting. "That'll be seventeen cents, sir. Fifteen for the first ten, then a cent a word after that. I'll have it done up right away, and the boy'll rush it over."

The message dispatched, Holmes took a place on the wooden bench that ran along one wall, and looked out at the bustling street through the plate-glass window fronting the office. The day had become brighter, and the sun glanced off the burnished wood and leather of cabs and private carriages, made more vivid the signs painted on the sides of drays and trucks, and sparkled metallically on the few automobiles which threaded their way among the horse-drawn vehicles which predominated. He was aware, as he had never been in London, of a torrent of vitality—crude, perhaps, but driving forward in some direction yet to be determined, harnessing the energy of machines and men in a partnership that would shape the new century.

A little oppressed by the scene outside, Holmes let his eyes rove around the telegraph office. They stopped at an advertising poster fastened to one wall, displaying the attraction to be found at the Hippodrome Theater. He gave a soundless whistle as he scanned one item:

Direct from the Palladium (in London):

The World-Famous

TWICKENHAM TOFFS

IN
BREATHTAKING ACROBATICS!

Sherlock Holmes' eyes gleamed. Another piece of the puzzle falling into place, and without any effort on his part!

"The Twickenham Toffs," he murmured. "Well,

well, what a mysterious, fascinating, and *tiny* world we live in, indeed!"

The boy who had departed five minutes before with Holmes' telegram came in through the street door and approached him, holding it.

"Sorry, Mister, the person's not there."

"How very odd," said Holmes cheerfully. "But, look here—it's marked urgent!"

"Yes, sir," the boy answered. "That's why they've given me the address of her boarding-house, so's I can deliver it there."

He displayed a penciled scrawl on the telegram's envelope.

"Splendid, splendid, my dear chap!" said Holmes. "I'll see to that myself, eh? Here you are!" He handed the youth a twenty-five-cent piece. As he turned to leave, he paused and added, "Now, you look like a lad who knows his way around this town. Where can I find a first-rate theatrical costumer?"

The messenger thought for a moment, and gave him an address only a few blocks distant. When their strange customer had left, the manager and the messenger looked at each other curiously.

"Full rates for a telegram that was never sent, and a big tip for *not* delivering it—there's a way to do business, Sully!" said the manager. "D'you suppose he's escaped from some asylum?"

The boy shrugged, and jingled his quarter against the few other coins in his pocket.

"An Englishman. You can't figure 'em out, no way!"

It was no more than an hour later that a closed four-wheeler with a battered trunk lashed to its top drew up in front of the Haymarket Hotel, an establishment in Forty-third Street, very much nearer to the North River than to Broadway, for all that its peeling sign announced that it catered to the theatrical profession.

The vehicle's lone passenger was just adjusting the last details of his appearance by fitting a spiky black wig to his head and capping it with a battered top hat, as the hack came to a halt.

The occupant, a tall, stout man clad in black and sporting a remarkable stand of mutton-chop whiskers and eyebrows, emerged from the carriage and pointed to the trunk atop it.

"'Ey, *signor carrozza!*" he called to the driver. "You bring-a in da *baule,* ha? And-a you handle wit' care, *si?* She's-a *molto* value, *capisc'?*"

The driver, who had taken many fares to the Haymarket in his time, and knew pretty accurately the kind of tip he could expect from actors, and from foreigners, and, most discouraging of all, from foreign actors, nodded gloomily and began undoing the securing ropes.

The passenger strode into the shabby lobby and up to the front desk, behind which a depressed-looking man stood peering down at some papers.

The newcomer struck an impressive attitude and fairly trumpeted, *"Buon giorno!"*

The man behind the counter started, and looked up.

"We presenting," said the apparition before him, *"Il Grande* Bandini! Direct-a from-a da Victoria Palace!"

"Victoria Palace, is it?" said the man. "I played there myself in years gone by, before I lost my wits and bought this place. What's your act, mate?"

"I . . . escape!"

"You escape?"

"Si! From-a da trunk, from-a da tank she's fill with water, from-a chains, from-a da locked-up cage—"

"But not from hotel bills, I hope," said the proprietor, not quite joking.

Bandini laughed uproariously.

The cab driver dropped the trunk—a massive one, at least five feet long—next to the desk, and said glumly, "That's a buck and a half, plus two bits for carting." If foreigners didn't see the point in tipping, a fellow might as well charge them something extra on the fare.

" 'Ere you are, my fine-a fellow," said the Great Bandini, counting out the precise amount mentioned into the outstretched hand. "And-a come to da Orpheum tomorrow night-a to watch-a me proform!"

The cab driver went out, something in his expression indicating that, on any visit to a performance of Bandini's, he would be well provided with a supply of elderly eggs.

"Playing the Orpheum, are you?" the proprietor asked. "How'd you hear about the Haymarket?"

"It was-a recommend me by a knife thrower I meet in Marseilles. A man-a, his name it was Nicholas Romaine."

"Don't seem to remember him. But we've got a *Miss* Romaine staying here now——her and her little boy." He gave a slight shrug. The "miss" might be a stage title, or it might not. The Haymarket was not the sort of place to ask to see marriage licenses. "Maybe they're related to your friend. I'll ask her when she comes in."

He glanced behind him at the honeycomb of room keys affixed to the wall.

"I can let you have a nice room on the third floor, number thirty-two." Hearing no objection, he took the key, opened the registration book and turned it toward Bandini. "If you'd care to register?" said he.

"Da room, she's-a clean? The Great Bandini, he don' share-a his bed-a with bugs!"

"Cleanest spot in town," said the proprietor flatly. "Ask anyone who lives here. *Front!*"

He gestured to a pair of bellboys to come over and take charge of the escape artist's trunk.

The Great Bandini signed the register with a flourish that sent a spray of ink drops on to the counter, and strode off to his room. The proprietor sighed, and dabbed at the spatter of tiny blots. Hardly any theater folks weren't strange in some way, he reflected, but this Bandini looked like being a real prize in the oddity line!

By about a half-hour after sunset, the proprietor felt confirmed in his opinion of his new guest. Instead of exploring the fleshpots of New York, resting in his room, or exchanging boastful stories with some of the other residents in the hotel's seedy bar, Bandini was in and out of the lobby constantly, appearing and disappearing like a jack-in-the-box. Finally, by early evening, he seemed to have settled into a chair in the corner, where he sat, apparently absorbed in a newspaper.

The proprietor looked up as the street door opened and a lithe young woman entered, carrying a string bag of groceries. He groaned a little at the sight of it. It was not that he really minded his guests doing a little clandestine cooking in their rooms—theater salaries didn't allow for much in the way of eating out—but there *was* a house rule, and her carrying the stuff in like that, out in the open, made it all the harder for him to crack down on the others when he wanted to. All the same, she was one of his favorites, and her youthful beauty brightened the dingy lobby.

"Ah, Miss Romaine!" he said, reaching for her key. He saw Bandini toss down his paper and start to rise from his chair. "By the way," he said, nodding to her, "over there's a gentleman who might be knowing a relation of yours."

Nicole Romaine swung around quickly, her eyes widening with fear. Bandini bounded across the room to her, seized her hand, and bent low over it.

"Signorina!" he bellowed. "I have had the *honore* of appearing on-a the same-a bill as you' *illustrioso* papa!" In softer tones, pitched to carry to her ears only, he said rapidly, "My name is Sherlock Holmes and if you value your life and your freedom, you will invite me to your room!"

Nicole Romaine's face was white and still as death for a moment. Then, slowly, she nodded.

Once inside the girl's shabby room, Holmes wasted no time in preliminaries.

"Where is the boy? Show him to me at once!" said he, his crisp tones contrasting oddly with his florid disguise.

"How did you know?" the girl gasped, still clearly in the grip of utmost dread.

"*Mademoiselle,* there is no time for that! *Where is he?*"

Holmes did not wait for her reply, but reached for the feebly burning gas jet protruding from the wall, and turned the handle sharply for a brighter flame. In the increased illumination, he immediately saw a moth-eaten couch in a corner of the room, and on it a form wrapped in a blanket.

Hurrying over to the couch, he kneeled beside it, drawing back the frayed fabric. The sleeping face he saw was unmistakably that in the photograph in Irene Adler's room. The stillness of that face, and the slow breathing, registered on his mind. He rose to face Nicole Romaine with a grimly accusing expression.

"He's drugged!"

The girl shrank back from his blazing stare.

"Only—only a few grains of laudanum, that's all, *monsieur,* and only when I must go out. I would not harm the boy!"

"You have assuredly harmed his mother! What brought you—his friend!—to take part in this outrage?"

The dancer sank into a rickety wooden chair and stared hopelessly at the worn carpeting.

"I had no choice. A man came to me three days ago . . . Charles Nickers, a tumbler with the Twickenham Toffs."

"Ah," said Holmes. "Yes, I had the distinct pleasure of arresting his brother, Bill, in London about two weeks ago. The Twickenham Toffs have long been part of Professor Moriarty's organization—but that's no matter to you, Miss Romaine. Now, what did this tumbler want of you?"

"He said . . . unless I did as I was bidden, my brother, Anatole, in Paris would be murdered!"

"I see. And what were your orders—in addition to persuading Scott Adler to take part in a prank directed at his governess?"

"To bring him here and engage a room facing the street. Originally, my room was in the rear. I was to say to the opera that I was ill. Then . . . twice a day I must inform Mr. Nickers that the boy is here and that no one had inquired after him."

"Inform him? By what means?"

"Each day, at eleven and again at six, he watches across the street. I open the curtain and nod. That is all."

Sherlock Holmes looked at his watch.

"Then it's almost time for him to be at his post," he murmured. He turned to the girl. *"Mademoiselle, you have received Moriarty's instructions. Now you shall hear mine! When your Charles Nickers arrives, you will give the proper signal, just as you've been told to do. And you will *continue* to give that signal twice a day until I relieve you of the responsibility. Do as I say, and you will emerge from this dismal matter unharmed, as will your brother. Fail me in any respect, Miss Nicole Romaine, and you will be held accountable for the death of Scott Adler!"

The girl shrank back appalled.

"Mon dieu!" she cried.

"Yes, I should have said exactly the same thing in your place, if I were French." Holmes nodded toward the window. "Is he out there?"

Nicole Romaine went to the window, drew the curtain, and looked into the street.

"If so," said Holmes, "give the signal."

The girl gave a simple slow inclination of her head, looked intently outwards for a moment, then stepped back and closed the curtain once again.

"He has gone."

"Good!" said Holmes. "Now . . ."

He eased the door to the room open and peered into the hallway, then pulled his own room key from his jacket pocket and handed it to the girl.

"I am in room thirty-two. Take the key. It is three doors along from you, on the opposite side of the corridor. Go and unlock the door. When the way is clear, signal to me. Now!"

Holmes opened the door wide enough for the girl to leave, and she slipped through it and hurried down the corridor. He kept watch on her as she came to the door of room 32, quickly opened it, and stepped inside. In a moment she emerged again, glanced in both directions, and gave him an urgent wave.

Sherlock Holmes turned to the sleeping boy on the couch, swept him up in his arms, and ran from the ballet dancer's room, covering the few yards' distance down the corridor in no more than two seconds.

Inside his own room, still holding the blanket-wrapped form of Scott Adler, Holmes faced Nicole Romaine and spoke urgently.

"Back to your room, *mademoiselle*, and remember, to do exactly as I say. This boy's *life* depends upon that!"

The girl clasped her hands in front of her and spoke fervently.

"Yes, yes! I will obey you utterly!"

"Do so!"

Sherlock Holmes gently kicked the door shut behind her and then laid the sleeping boy down on the bed. The large trunk which had accompanied "Bandini" to the hotel stood in the center of the floor, and Holmes knelt by it and opened it. Inside was a network of intertwined ropes attached to the sides and ends of the trunk, forming a hammock, on which rested some folded blankets and leather straps. On it Holmes now placed Scott Adler, cushioning him with the blankets and securing him in place with the straps. Taking out his pocket-knife, he opened the awl blade it contained, and tested the clusters of small holes unobtrusively bored near the handles of the trunk. Satisfied that the supply of air would be sufficient, he closed the trunk.

"You'll have a bruise or two to show for your

adventure, lad," he said softly, "but they'll soon disappear under your mother's kisses."

He snapped shut the two brass locks that secured the trunk, and turned a key in both. Straightening up, he inspected himself in the tarnished mirror that hung over the battered chest-of-drawers, and made small adjustments to his wig and clothing. Next, he took a deep breath, flung the door open, and strode into the corridor and down it to the open stairwell.

Leaning over the railing, he bellowed down to the lobby two flights below, *"Signore!"*

In a moment, he could see the foreshortened figure of the proprietor beneath him, staring up in surprise.

"This is not an *albergo* for actors, it is a pen-a for pigs! Send-a up for my luggage and-a prepare my bill!"

Along the corridor in which he now stood, and on the floors above and below him, Holmes could hear the sound of doors being cautiously opened, and was aware of heads poking curiously out behind him. Good: the proprietor would be all the more concerned to be rid of the Great Bandini with no more fuss than was already being made, and would have no time to perceive the fact that Bandini's trunk was noticeably heavier than when it had been brought in.

He raised his voice to an enraged howl.

"I will not-a spend five-a more minutes in this-a place!"

It was no more, in fact, than four minutes before Holmes, the trunk carefully set on the seat facing him, was in a cab, his hotel bill paid to the white-faced proprietor, and on his way to the Algonquin Hotel.

Chapter Eleven

Sherlock Holmes had made it clear that no results could be expected from his efforts during the daylight hours, and had laid no injunction upon myself or Irene Adler save that we be at her residence from six o'clock onwards.

The lady herself, the outward shell of Holmes with which she had gulled our watchers now being restored to the wardrobe at the hotel, expressed no wish but to return home.

"I am in no mood for diversion, or even company, Dr. Watson," said she. "I have often been alone and have grown accustomed to it, but am rarely lonely. This will be a long day, and I shall wish for nothing so much as the setting of the sun, whatever it may bring, but I do not require or wish companionship. Cast yourself loose in this great city, and discover what you may of what it has to offer; I, on my part, may be cheered to think of the experiences you will have, and shall look forward to hearing your account of them."

I thought that a most handsome dismissal, and confess I was relieved to have it made so clear that my company was not wanted. Miss Adler is a fine figure of a woman, no doubt of that, but more intense and high-powered than I find comfortable for any extended period.

Having seen her into a cab, then, I found myself with the better part of a spring day in New York to spend as I would, it then being only ten o'clock.

I am afraid that, in the event, I did not make the

best use of it. In vain to ask me of the treasures of the Metropolitan Museum of Art, the wonders of the Natural History Museum, the magnificent view of the city to be obtained from the torch of the Statue of Liberty—even the more worldly delights of Koster & Bial's "improper Vaudeville" and certain "joints" in Thirty-third and Fifty-seventh Streets where opium may be freely smoked, about which not a few loudly dressed individuals I encountered in my wanderings seemed anxious to inform me. I did, indeed, in a trip up Fifth Avenue in an electric omnibus, the open back of which afforded an incomparable view of a mile or more of millionaires' palatial residences, *glimpse* the famed art museum, but did not enter it. I did have a moment of disorientation when observing what appeared to be Cleopatra's Needle, so familiar to me in London, poking out of the trees behind the museum, but was informed that it was that obelisk's twin, presented to New York by the Khedive of Egypt some twenty-five years past.

What I did, in fact, once I had taken care of the one task I had promised myself to complete—the purchase of a necktie or so, more in keeping with the tone of the New World—was to abandon myself to the city, let myself drift about it as freely as a balloon, with not even the directing intelligence that Mr. Santos-Dumont brings to aerial navigation. A wanderer may not see everything that the shepherded tourist does, but he will see other things of equal interest, and remember them the better for having been surprised by them.

The desk clerk at the Algonquin, agreeing perhaps too readily that I would do well to invest in some more colorful neckwear, suggested that I try the Windsor Arcade, which contains a number of shops of all sorts, and fronts on Fifth Avenue only a few streets north of that in which the hotel stands. Arriving there, I was agreeably surprised to find it remarkably similar to the Burlington Arcade in Piccadilly, though more restrained in its style of architecture. There was indeed an excellent haberdasher's along its central corridor, and I treated myself to a quarter-dozen of ties, one of a positively alarming electric-blue hue which, it seemed to me, might very nearly serve to light my way through a London fog.

Having paid for the ties, I told the salesman I was staying at the Algonquin Hotel.

"I am happy to hear that," he observed. "It is said to be a swell place."

He then wrapped the ties in a neat parcel and pushed them across the counter to me. I placed my forefinger on the parcel and pushed it back to his side of the counter.

"It's the Algonquin," said I. "Dr. John Watson."

"I myself am Arnold Bozeman," said he, and, with his own forefinger returned the ball, as it were, to my court.

"These are to go to the Algonquin Hotel!" I moved the parcel yet again.

"I am sure they will be worthy of their surroundings," said the salesman—not, this time, touching the package, but instead placing his hands behind his back.

The meaning of his words and actions finally became clear to me.

"Do you mean you do not deliver purchases made here?"

"No, sir. Our customers tend to that, at least with small parcels."

I was appalled.

"Surely . . . you don't expect me to carry a shop package . . . in the *street?*"

Mr. Bozeman looked at me closely.

"I perceive you are English, sir." I admitted it. He gave a sigh. "This store has its policy. The custom of the country is to carry off what one has bought unless it is a considerable burden. Yesterday J. P. Morgan himself trotted out with a vest we had renewed the white piping on, nicely wrapped up in brown paper. Yet . . . you are English, and I have argued with Englishmen on such points before. I will deliver your ties to the hotel myself during the very short time I am allowed for my lunch."

I thanked him and left the store, pleased to have encountered an example of the warmth and consideration which the American merchant brings to his business.

On Fifth Avenue, I hailed a northward-bound electric omnibus, as I have said, and took my seat in one of the eight outside places. The silent, steady ride was a novelty to me, and the dazzling variety of buildings on both sides of the Avenue drew my attention constantly.

By the time we reached a point somewhat north of the Metropolitan Museum, however, I found myself out of sorts. For very nearly two miles, I saw no building that was not the residence of a millionaire, and, even though the title referred to fortunes reckoned in dollars rather than pounds, it was beyond me what so many people might be doing that was worth so much. I am in general well content with the order of things, but there are some aspects of society the conservative man who wishes to remain so would do well to avoid.

I abandoned the omnibus and struck eastward, still surprised at being able to see so far along any one street. I walked for a while in the shadow of the elevated railway at Third Avenue, much taken with the jumble of old houses, shops, and open land. A taint carried in the wind told me that a slaughterhouse was not far away, reminding me of my student days at Bart's, cheek by jowl with the Smithfields abattoirs.

It may have been because my mind was turning in that direction that I was struck by the name over a pawnbroker's establishment on the avenue: A. HANZÄHNE. Scarcely a common name, surely, yet one I had encountered in London, and there belonging to a pawnbroker as well, an estimable fellow in the Marylebone High Street who had often passed along information useful to Sherlock Holmes. Might this not be a relative, emigrated to the New World?

I entered the shop, introduced myself to the proprietor, and found that he was indeed first cousin to my old acquaintance. I gave him the latest news of his kinsman and of the old country, and we chatted most pleasantly a moment or so.

He eventually moved away from me to attend to a customer, a young woman of good appearance though obviously not affluent. After the transaction, he returned, shaking his head.

"A sad business, Doctor," said he. "There's a young lady, a real trump, married just a year to a nice fellow. They're as much in love as you ever remember being when you were twenty—and more. But times is hard, and they've got no money. She's just pawned the last good piece of jewelry she had from her mother—been in the family for generations—to buy her husband something for the anniversary present. I gave her what I could, but God knows if she can ever redeem the piece."

Before we had got fairly started on renewing our conversation, he was called away again, this time to deal with a young man.

"If that don't beat all," he remarked when the business was done. "Now, that's the husband of the girl that was just in. And wouldn't you know he's hocked a set of gold medals he won for swimming at college—to buy his lady something for the anniversary?"

"As you said, a sad business," I commented.

He shrugged.

"Listen, maybe wanting to *give* somebody something is better than *having* something, who's to say?"

I took my adieux, promising to give his cousin in London word of our meeting, and went on my way.

It seemed to me best to strike back toward a less dingy part of the city, and I was making my way in the direction of Fifth Avenue once more, when I heard a confused babble of cries, in which I could clearly make out the words "Help!" and "Doctor!" Through the noise, a terrified, inhuman squealing arose. I ran across to a crowd I saw gathering around the door of a shop, and pushed my way through, saying as authoritatively as I could, "I am a doctor!"

It was not, however, a human being that stood in need of my services.

A well-fed and cared-for, but certainly mongrel dog, was cruelly imprisoned in a strange manner. An iron grillwork in front of the shop was secured to a metal post by a length of chain and a padlock; and there had evidently been just enough slack in the chain for the animal to get its head wedged through it in such a manner that it could not withdraw it. This may have been the result of an injudicious leap, for the poor brute was nearly suspended in the air, with only its hind feet touching the pavement, and must soon perish of slow strangulation.

The crowd was alive with suggestions and comment. Listening to these, I soon learned that the owner of the shop was away and could not be reached; that no one had the key to the padlock; and that it had been generally agreed that any attempt to break the chain with a cold chisel would break the dog's neck before serving its purpose. A tearful small girl standing by and sobbing was evidently the dog's owner, and it kept looking at her desperately as though for some last chance of help.

The girl pulled urgently at the sleeve of a burly man next to her.

"Help him, Brynie. You c'n do it—you know you c'n do it! Please!"

"Nit!" said the man she addressed, looking nervously at a policeman who had joined the crowd. "You know I can't do dat—not now!"

"But you *got* to. Treff's *dying,* an' there's nobody—!"

"I can't—an' shut up dat talk!"

I could see that the policeman was looking at the man as if he knew him well.

The girl stopped her sobbing and looked up at him. Her face was still, and very old, suddenly.

"Oh . . . yeah. He's a . . . a dog, that's all. It don't matter, I guess."

"Oh, *hell!*"

The man darted an agonized glance at the policeman, reached for the padlock, and, with a few deft movements of his fingers, had it open. The dog dropped to the ground, and he and the little girl were a sudden joyous tangle of fur and shabby skirts.

The policeman moved up to the dog's rescuer.

"Pretty clever fingers you got, Brynie," I heard him murmur.

"Yeah, Riley." The man's shoulders slumped.

"Opened that lock as neat as the fellow that went into Meyer's market, and the tailor shop, and opened the safe in the back room of the Shamrock—and him doing it all in one week," observed the officer.

"Yeah, Riley."

"Well." The policeman cocked his helmeted head and looked at the man. "Now, that's a low class of goings-on, isn't it," said he. "A man that'd take . . . well, a lot of trouble to save a little girl's dog . . . I don't think he'd be the kind that would do the kind of thing I'm talking of, would you? Not considering the past so much as what's to come, if you take my meaning."

With dawning hope, the man Brynie looked at the officer, then nodded vigorously, and darted off.

I saw other curious and striking things during the remainder of the day, but was most struck by an incident at the Central Park Zoo, where I found myself in mid-afternoon, contemplating a polar bear and wondering why it persisted in swinging its head back and forth like an animated toy.

There came an outcry next to me, and, turning, I perceived a boy of perhaps ten, a sullen expression on his fat face, kicking a man who was holding him by the hand. I should have taken them for father and son, except that the boy was overdressed to a degree, in velvet knee-breeches and jacket and patent-leather shoes, and the man, who had the appearance of an out-of-work clerk, was verging on shabbiness.

As I watched this curious drama, the man's face brightened, in spite of the pain occasioned by the kicks now landing regularly on his shins and ankles, and he called out to a fashionably dressed man of about twenty sauntering nearby, "Sir! Sir!"

The young fellow turned, and an expression of weary distaste crossed his face. Reluctantly, he approached the odd pair.

"I saw you earlier with your brother, sir," the shabby man said, "and when I noticed the lad wandering by himself, I ventured to take hold of him and seek you out."

"Decent of you," the young man responded gloomily.

"Um . . . now that I have restored him to you, as it were . . . I wonder if some pecuniary recognition might not be in order?"

The shabby man smiled ingratiatingly. The young man looked at his brother and shuddered.

"Very well," he replied. "Tell you what. I don't want to do you down, so how about you handing over two dollars, and I'll take him back off your hands. Fair?"

As I left the scene, the shabby man looked torn between disappointed anger and a serious consideration of the proposition.

The sun was beginning to decline, and I thought it best to make my way toward Gramercy Park, to be sure of being there at the appointed time. The elevated train, however, which I took in a spirit of daring, and which afforded me a remarkable new perspective on the city, whisked me downtown far faster than I expected, leaving me another half-hour or so if I wished to use it. I had eaten little and, passing an establishment calling itself Viemeister's, from which came a pleasant scent of food and good beer, I stepped inside.

Though primarily a barroom, it had much of the atmosphere of some of our London public-houses, with an etched glass mirror behind the long, dark bar, and much wood panelling throughout. I did not care to sit at the bar, and found a booth with two padded benches in it vacant, one of a row on the wall opposite the bar. One indication that I was in the mechanized New World rather than the Old, was a push-button let into the wall above the table that occupied the space between the two benches. I pushed it, and in a moment a waiter appeared to take my order for a glass of ale and a meat sandwich of some kind.

"Whatever your cook does best, eh?" said I.

The sandwich, when it came, consisted of a prodigious amount of a highly spiced meat, remarkably pungent in aroma, between two slices of a dark and rather tough bread. It was all unfamiliar, but I was footsore and hungry, and the "pastromy," as the waiter called it, went extraordinarily well with the rather over-chilled ale.

" 'Scuse me, sir."

I looked up to see a stocky man, a few years younger than myself, with a plump face and thinning, curly hair, standing in the aisle next to the booth. He was carrying a large glass of lager and a plate laden with several different sorts of delicacy.

"Would I be imposing if I shared the booth?" he asked in accents which retained a touch of the American South, or possibly West, in their softness. "The others are taken, and I don't cotton to the bar. It's too easy to fall off one of those stools."

I indicated, with a gesture, that he was welcome. I had spoken to scarcely anyone that day, and, still savoring my holiday from the pressing concerns that had brought Holmes and myself to the city, was glad of the chance to prolong it for a few moments of casual conversation.

"Actually," said my new companion, seating himself, "I wanted to get a good look at a paying customer for the kitchen. Most everybody that comes in here dives into the free lunch."

He indicated his heaped plate.

"I wasn't aware that there was such a thing as a free lunch," said I.

"There ain't, but it's like perpetual motion. There's a powerful lot of people think they can find it, and keep looking."

It was clear that I had happened upon an original —or he upon me—and I greatly enjoyed our half-hour of talk. My new friend had a vast fund of information and anecdote upon many topics: the Far West, prison life, revolutions and curious customs in Central America. But his main love seemed to be the city of New York.

"It's the new Arabian Nights," he assured me. "Haroun-al-Raschid and his Baghdad aren't in the game, alongside Gotham."

"Well once you've got your Underground completed, I suppose you could call it Baghdad-on-the-Subway," said I.

"Say, so you could!" said the man opposite me.

Having regaled me so entertainingly, he now attempted to draw me out in exchange, and I found myself somewhat at a loss. The delicate matter of the kidnapping of Scott Adler, to say nothing of the missing gold from Mr. McGraw's Exchange, were certainly not to be bandied about in idle talk; and the very fact that Sherlock Holmes and his associate and chronicler were in the city would be bound to excite speculation of the most troublesome kind, if it became known. I must, therefore, remain incognito. It followed that much that I had to tell that might have interested my companion could not be referred to. I turned the conversation to my experiences of the day in the city, ordinary though they had been.

He was fascinated by the story of my encounter with the pawnbroker Hahnzähne, though it seemed to me nothing remarkable that a man in London should have a cousin in New York; his eyes went positively round at the business of the trapped dog; and the sad narrative of the unnatural fellow at the zoo who cheated his brother's rescuer out of his due reward seemed to strike him as hugely funny.

"Say, if you were a writer," said he, "you'd have

just about paid for your trip from England with those. Lord! I don't know when I've come across story material like that!"

"Well, I do write now and then," I ventured, for a moment forgetting my resolve to avoid revealing my identity. "But I don't see any possibilities in what I've told you. I mean, they're the kind of thing that happens in your city—every day, I'm sure—and nothing to take notice of, unless you're a foreigner wandering about."

He cocked his head at me and took a sip from his mug of lager.

"A writer. What's your line?"

"Detective stories," I said, with some reluctance.

Sherlock Holmes might have spun some convincing tale under those circumstances—and would very likely have not got into them at all—but I found it impossible to answer a direct question with an outright lie.

"Hm. And, sir, your name is . . . ?"

"Watson."

"I was beginning to think it might be. Mine's Porter, W. S.—W. for William, which I don't use, S. for Sydney, also retired, and Porter for Porter, which has been scratched at the starting gate. Say, Watson, if that's the straight goods about your doing the 'Lo! the poor Indian' act with those pearls richer than all your tribe you were telling me about, d'you mind if I pick 'em up and string 'em together?"

As far as I could tell from his odd mixture of slang and literary allusion, he seemed to be requesting permission to make literary use of the banal anecdotes I had recounted. I granted it gladly, and, seeing that the sun had nearly set, rose and prepared to take my leave.

"I shall scan the magazines with interest to see what you have been able to make of my poor experiences, Mr. Porter," said I.

"Well, you won't get far if you run your thumb down the index under P," said he. "I use a pen name

—and I'm here to tell you that them that lives in the pen can live *by* the pen."

This example of American allusive humor escaped me, I confess, but Mr. Porter confided his pseudonym in me, and I left, hastening to arrive at Irene Adler's house in good time, pondering on what curious significance he might place on it.

Henry is, of course, an honored name, our nation having had eight kings so styled. But what was the point of prefacing it with the single initial, reminding one of nothing so much as the zero, of O?

Chapter Twelve

It was but a few moments' walk from the Viemeister tavern in Eighteenth Street to number 4, Gramercy Park West, and I was there before the last rays of the setting sun had ceased from gilding the buildings on the northern side of the square.

The next hour or so was one of the least comfortable periods of my life. Though calm, Irene Adler was keyed up to a kind of tense stillness, and was in no mood for conversation. Her whole being seemed concentrated on awaiting the issue of Sherlock Holmes' efforts that day. I sat in one chair, then another; looked at a newspaper and at a magazine; admired a vase on the mantel and a porcelain shepherdess on a small table; and consulted my watch each half-hour or so, as it seemed, although the hands usually proved to have moved no more than ten or twelve minutes each time. Heller's appearance with a pot of tea and some sweet biscuits cheered me up, after an hour of this atmosphere, as much as might one of those roistering banquets Dickens describes so vividly.

It was close upon eight o'clock when the jangle of the doorbell brought Irene Adler and myself to our feet. As I descended the stairs, I saw Heller opening the door to admit a tall fellow in chauffeur's livery and peaked cap, sporting a giant handlebar moustache.

As though he entertained doubts of Heller's hearing, he boomed at him in a voice loud enough to carry into the street, "Mr. Holmes' and Dr. Watson's luggage from the hotel! Come on and give me a hand with it!"

I descended the stairs and inquired, "Good heavens, what's this about?"

"I said," bawled the man, "I've got Mr. Holmes' and Dr. Watson's luggage, like you ordered, and I need some help getting it in the house!"

Heller looked questioningly at his mistress.

"Help the man carry in the luggage, Heller," said she, calmly.

"Yes, ma'am."

The butler joined the uniformed man on the steps outside.

"What's our luggage being brought here for, anyway?" I wondered.

"I'm sure we'll find out very soon," said Irene Adler.

Peering outside into the street, I saw a carriage by the curb—and, beyond it, I fancied, a light blob against the darkness of the park trees that might well have been our checked-suited spy. Through the open door of the carriage I observed a number of familiar suitcases and a large trunk that had *not,* I knew, formed part of our effects on the trip from England. As I watched, the uniformed man pulled out two of the suitcases and handed them to Heller, who trotted up into the lobby with them and set them down.

I looked at the nearest.

"Mine, right enough," said I, and picked it up. "Bless my soul—it's empty!" Now quite alarmed at this turn of events, I turned to the uniformed man as he entered with two more suitcases, and cried, "Look here, my good man—"

"There's quite a large trunk in the carriage, Watson." Sherlock Holmes' precise tones cut off my protest. "As soon as Heller and I have it halfway across the sidewalk so that it's blocking the view of that chap across the street, I want you to get into that carriage as fast as you can and lie on the floor. Under no circumstances allow yourself to be seen."

"Holmes!" I exclaimed, dropping the empty suitcase.

"Remember to do exactly as I say!"

He turned and descended the outside stairs once more. I looked in perplexity at Irene Adler, who appeared, as always, calm—and now ready to play her part, whatever it might be.

I turned to look again through the outer door. Holmes and Heller were now removing the trunk from the carriage.

I heard Holmes call out, "Careful now, buddy."

Irene Adler placed one hand firmly on my arm. As they reached the bottom of the steps, she tightened her grip for an instant and said, urgently, *"Now,* Dr. Watson!"

Crouching low and using the trunk as a screen, I scuttled down the steps and flung myself into the carriage, stretching out face down upon the floor, where I stayed during stirring events of the next few moments within the house, of which I learned only later.

Once the trunk had been brought into the foyer and the door tight closed behind it, Holmes lost no time in unlocking and opening it.

As the lid rose, revealing the sleeping boy, Irene Adler's eyes widened, and she gave a low cry of relief and joy: "Scott!"

She fell to her knees beside the trunk, her head bowed, as Holmes quickly undid the straps that had kept the boy secure during his jolting journeys. As he did so, Scott stirred and opened his eyes.

"Mother?" said he bewilderedly. "How'd I get here?" He felt the metal edges of the trunk in wonder and confusion. "What's this? Where's Nicole?"

His mother was now weeping and clasping him to her.

"Oh, Scott, Scott, Scott!"

Holmes, still on his knees beside the trunk, regarded them gravely for a moment, then stood up. Irene Adler looked into his face, and seemed about to press him for an explanation of the miracle that had befallen her and her son.

"Sherlock . . . ?"

"I've no time now," said Holmes. "If I'm in here

too long—" He gave a meaningful jerk of his head in the direction of the spot where Moriarty's spy kept his vigil. Then he patted Scott Adler on the head and smiled. "Lad's as fit as a fiddle. But, Irene, matters remain grave. I must ask you under no circumstances to stir from the house or let the boy be seen, until I give the word."

"Of course."

Sherlock Holmes turned to Heller.

"Open the door," he instructed. The butler did so, and Holmes, standing out of any view from outside, called, in his own voice, "Thank you, my man! Here's something for your pains!"

He then moved smartly out on to the front steps, replying to himself in his delivery-man's boom, "Thank you, sir. Thank you very much!"

In a moment he had clambered up on to the driver's seat of the carriage, whipped up the horse, and driven off. As the vehicle began to move, I eased myself from the floor and looked cautiously out the back window. I could see the man in the checked suit moving hastily away from his post, and, opening the hatchway at the front of the carriage, I passed this news to Holmes.

"Naturally enough, Watson," said he. "He is even now getting word to his master that you and I have moved, bag and baggage, into the house of Miss Irene Adler—and it is there that his attention will be focussed for the next few all-important days!"

"By George, you're right, Holmes," said I a short time later in our rooms at the Algonquin, as I looked out the window into the street. "Not a sign of anyone watching us!"

Sherlock Holmes, rubbing briskly at a last wisp of false moustache clinging to his upper lip, emerged from the bedroom.

"I assumed as much, Watson," he replied. "We

have them round now—and they don't know it. It's *our* game from here on."

"What's the next move, then?"

"Dinner, I should say. It's almost on nine; and I have not dined, Watson, I have not lunched, and I've only the vaguest memory of having breakfasted. I suggest we make up for that lapse in the Algonquin's most estimable restaurant, and look up Inspector Lafferty as soon after that as we're able."

"Hear, hear!" said I. "I suggest you ask for some pastromy. It's a remarkable local dish, and certainly a hotel named for one of the aboriginal tribes ought to be able to provide the native foods."

We found Inspector Lafferty at his office, and, to his credit, he wasted no time in further recriminations or in requiring explanations of Holmes' decision to reverse his stand on participating in the investigation of the gold theft. He quickly arranged for us to meet Mr. Mortimer McGraw the next day at the Bouwerie National Bank, to inspect the scene of the crime.

It certainly seemed an unlikely crime to have taken place. The entrance to the lift leading down to the vaults was secured by a combination lock, as were the controls of the lift itself.

Holmes inspected the lift with keen interest as he and I, McGraw, and Lafferty entered it, and said, "I presume the lock on the controls has a different combination from the one that unlocks the main door?"

"It does, sir," said McGraw.

"How many people know these combinations?"

"Only the six employees of the exchange and myself. I might also add that the tumblers are changed every three months."

The controls unlocked, Mr. McGraw tugged on a handle, and the lift began to move downwards.

"Admirable," said Holmes. *"If* in this case futile. Is this the only way in which the vaults can be reached?"

"Up until five days ago it was," Inspector Lafferty observed bitterly.

With the Inspector and McGraw sunk in gloom, and myself at sea, only Holmes seemed perfectly at ease, looking about the lift as if memorizing the details of its operation.

"What sort of lift is this?" said he.

"Drum and cable," replied McGraw. "Works from above."

"And how far do we descend?"

"One hundred and fifty feet."

"At what rate of speed?"

"Two hundred feet a minute."

Not for the first time, I felt a sense of impatience with Sherlock Holmes' passion for facts. It was all very well for him to be able to know the number of steps in any staircase he used, and similar parlor-tricks, but to continue this jackdaw accumulation of statistics whilst his mind should have been puzzling out the means of the theft of milliards (if that *is* what billions are) of dollars' worth of gold—that smacked of frivolity.

A jolt signalled the end of our descent.

"Ah, we appear to have arrived," said Holmes.

McGraw slid back the iron-mesh inner doors of the lift, revealing yet another door of solid steel. This, too, was equipped with a combination lock, which he proceeded to manipulate while Holmes watched.

"I take it that this combination also differs from its fellows, and is altered every ninety days as well?"

"Correct, sir." McGraw pushed open the heavy door, and gave a mournful sigh. "And now, Mr. Holmes, I ask you to see for yourself what I can only describe as the most dismal sight the world has ever seen."

It was certainly a strange spectacle. On either side of a central corridor hewn from the living rock stood rows of cells, uncannily like those in a jail, with their barred doors all standing open, as though there had been a mass release, or escape, of prisoners. A row of electric bulbs set into the ceiling of the corridor formed a line that led to the far end and revealed a jagged patch of blackness in the back wall: the hole that had been blasted in it. Holmes made his way to this, and fell to examining it with his magnifying glass.

After a moment, he looked at McGraw, and remarked, "Extraordinary. More than a foot of rock and concrete had to be cut through. The noise must have been deafening."

"Since they've been working on the subway, you could set off dynamite and no one would hear it," said McGraw.

"A condition that doubtless was taken advantage of."

Holmes stepped through the hole into the tunnel leading to the subway excavation, and moved slowly along it. Lafferty, McGraw, and I stared after him, able to make him out only vaguely in the darkness as he descended at a distinct angle.

He called back to us over his shoulder, "Two pieces of bullion were left behind, you say? Where?"

Inspector Lafferty pointed past Holmes and shouted, "One in the tunnel just ahead of you, the other about fifty feet south of the main excavation."

Sherlock Holmes turned and started back toward where we stood. As he approached, I ventured a comment.

"Well, that makes it clear enough, doesn't it, Holmes? They made off in that direction with their boodle."

"One would immediately accept that conclusion, Watson, I quite agree," said he, stepping through the breached wall once again. "I should like a closer look at these vaults now."

We stood aside and he prowled along the opened cells like a terrier questing among rat-holes in a barn to see if any of them holds a quarry. He ventured into one of the cells in the middle of the line, and his voice, given a hollow, echoing quality by the confined space, came out to us: "How many actual *bars* of gold were stored here, do you know?"

Mr. McGraw answered, "Just prior to the theft these vaults held eighteen million pounds of gold, consisting of three hundred and sixty thousand fifty pound blocks, each valued at twenty-eight thousand dollars."

Holmes' head popped out of the cell he was inspecting. He stared hard at the president of the Exchange.

"Three hundred sixty thousand blocks? And they were shifted out of here without anyone noticing it? I believe I would not be putting it too strongly to say that is a remarkable circumstance, gentlemen!"

I looked at him closely. When that mild, almost playful tone came into his voice, it was a clear sign that Sherlock Holmes believed he had a card or so up his sleeve.

Inspector Lafferty's reaction was to snort, while Mortimer McGraw said impatiently, "Remarkable! If we weren't standing here looking at these empty vaults, I'd say it was impossible!"

"Yes" said Holmes. "I should say so, too." He gave a final look around at the vaults. "I should like to return to the lift now."

Once there, he pointed to a small trap door in the ceiling of the lift.

"That hatchway there. Does it provide access to the overhead drum and cable?"

"Yes," answered McGraw.

"Watson, might I trouble you for a leg up?"

"Of course. Here you are," said I, and formed a stirrup with my hands.

Holmes stepped on to it, and with the increased distance from the floor, was able to open the trap door, then hoist himself partway through the hatchway by grasping its sides. His voice, muffled by the ceiling, came back to us.

"Very sensible of you, Mr. McGraw, to have the drum housing illuminated by electricity. Very convenient for repairs, I'm sure; and it always helps to shed light on things."

McGraw was beginning to have a sour look, as though he had come to question the value of Sherlock Holmes' help in the case. Meanwhile, the detective dropped back to the lift floor.

"Thank you. I think I've seen everything I need to see, gentlemen. I have one final inquiry to make elsewhere, following which I believe I shall be able to fit all the pieces together and provide you with a satisfactory solution."

McGraw seemed taken aback at this display of confidence.

"And the gold?" he inquired.

"The gold, of course, will be forthcoming with the solution of the problem."

Inspector Lafferty appeared to be evenly divided between disbelief and hope.

"In time for the transfer of the bullion tomorrow morning?" he asked.

Holmes gave him a cheerful smile, and said, "It is my fondest wish."

He amiably fended off any further questions, and, once back at the street level of the bank, we took our leave of two sorely confused men.

Holmes set off at a brisk pace through lower Manhattan, a section which, except for the height of the buildings, might almost have been London. It had many winding streets, some of them even bearing familiar names, such as Maiden Lane, and I was given quite a turn when I saw a church that might have been twin to St. Martin's-in-the-Fields.

My friend appeared to have a definite destination in mind, and I asked, "Where are we off to now?"

"To pay a call on Thomas Vallence and Company, the firm that designed the underground. I want to ascertain the depth of the excavation at the point at which it passed the Bouwerie National Bank. I shall be most astonished if we are not told that the figure is precisely one hundred fifty feet."

The engineers at the Vallence office proved most cooperative; and so did their blueprints and field notes, which bore out Holmes' estimate of the excavation's depth precisely.

I knew well enough by now that my friend's interest in this measurement was not another example of his mania for general information—and must bear importantly on the case. Yet I could not see how. I puzzled over this for a space, as we jogged northward in a cab—Holmes had flatly rejected my suggestion that we return uptown via the elevated railway—and finally gave it up.

"Just what is it we have found out?" I asked.

"Everything."

"*Everything?* You mean you know where the gold is?"

"I knew *that* the moment we descended in the lift. I merely wanted to double-check my certainty."

"Well . . . where is it?"

"We were standing on it."

"We were— *Holmes!*"

So bizarre a statement must be a joke, yet I could not make out the point of it.

"Don't you see what the wily devil has done, man?"

I felt distinctly put out. "No, I *don't* see. And I'm sure I should be delighted if you'd tell me!"

Holmes sprawled in the seat, legs outstretched and feet resting on the opposite bench, his fingers steepled.

"Consider, Watson. Three hundred sixty thousand blocks of gold, each weighing fifty pounds. Give Moriarty a hundred—give him *two* hundred—men, each able to carry a fifty-pound block of gold."

"Very well. What then?"

"Each of those two hundred men would have to carry eighteen hundred blocks out of those vaults."

At this point we arrived at the hotel, and continued the conversation while entering it, traversing the lobby, and regaining our rooms.

"To carry a single fifty-pound block from the vaults, through the tunnel to some conveyance waiting in the excavation, and then to return for a second block, could not reasonably be accomplished in less than ten minutes. In other words, Watson, it would take eighteen *thousand* minutes, or three hundred *hours* to complete the task. That's over twelve days—and the gold was there six days ago!"

A quick calculation seemed to indicate that the only way the crime could have been accomplished was with the aid of an army of five hundred men working twenty-four hours a day. But I could see no point whatever in saying so.

"Mr. McGraw's instincts were quite correct," said Holmes. "The task appears impossible, in spite of the evidence of the empty vaults."

"But, Holmes, they *were* empty!"

Now back in our sitting room, he removed his cloak and cap and reached for his pipe.

"*Those* vaults were," he said.

"Those vaults? Holmes, what on earth are you suggesting?"

"Watson, I asked how far down the lift went. I was told one hundred fifty feet. That means the vaults must be one hundred fifty feet below the bank. But the depth of the subway excavation at that point was *also* one hundred fifty feet. When I looked up at the overhead cable while the lift was presumably at the bottom of the shaft, I could see several coils of it wound round the drum at the top; if inspected on the spot, I dare say one would find about fifteen feet of it."

He lit the pipe and puffed out a cloud of pungent blue smoke.

"Mr. McGraw told me," he continued, "that the rate of descent was two hundred feet a minute, meaning it should have taken the lift forty-five seconds to reach the vaults. It took thirty-nine. And I am sure you noticed that the tunnel from the vaults to the excavation slopes *downwards!*"

"Why, so it does! Then—"

"Watson, there is only one inescapable conclusion. The vaults we examined were *not* the vaults containing the gold. They were an exact replica built directly *above* the actual vaults. It will be discovered, I am confident, when the floor of the lift is removed, that iron bars will have been inserted into the shaft to prevent the lift descending the remaining ten feet to the actual vaults—where all of the gold still safely resides!"

Chapter Thirteen

Sherlock Holmes had laid it all out clearly and, as he had said, the conclusion was inescapable. Nevertheless, it was still hard to credit.

"But, Holmes, the vault door, the combination lock—the cages themselves—*everything?*"

"Duplicated down to the smallest detail. Some member of Mr. McGraw's staff has thrown in his lot with Moriarty and provided him with all the necessary details."

"It must have taken months!"

"Yes! And with so many hundreds of men employed in construction of the underground, who would notice a handful of Moriarty's cohorts tunnelling for purposes of their own?"

Hands behind my back, I paced the room, pondering this incredible, but moment by moment more convincing, solution. I then turned to Holmes, who was lounging comfortably and puffing at his pipe.

"One thing, Holmes," said I. "You were quite certain of all this while we were still with Inspector Lafferty. Yet you said nothing. Why?"

Sherlock Holmes' expression grew grave, and he removed the pipe from his mouth.

"I still fear for the boy's life."

"But he's safe at hime now!" I protested.

"Safe only so long as Moriarty thinks him still a prisoner. Tomorrow's newspapers hold the key. If the theft is reported, he will know that I have obeyed his orders, and it will be safe to release Scott. If the financial page carries news of the exchange transaction, he will know I have tricked him, and he will hasten to seize the boy from Mademoiselle Romaine. He will learn that I have forestalled him, and his rage will be towering. He will not rest until he has had his revenge on me—through Scott!"

He rose and paced the room, and I stood to one side in order to avoid getting in his way.

"I must know where Moriarty is," he said, "and he must be in the custody of the police, before I can safely reveal the location of the gold. No other course of action is permissible!"

"Perhaps so," I replied, "but how on earth do you expect to manage that? It took you half a year to ferret out the man's lodgings in Limehouse."

Sherlock Holmes regarded me for a moment, appearing to ponder deeply. Then a smile lit up his face.

"I'm not too proud to learn, Watson. Why not employ the methods *he* used in ferreting *me* out?"

He started for the door, taking up his cloak and cap once more.

"Here—where are you going?" I called.

He paused with his hand on the doorknob.

"Back to that most admirable establishment, the Eaves Costume Company!"

Then he was gone.

Alone in the hotel room, I wondered what strange role he would assume this time. It could hardly be more bizarre than that of the Great Bandini!

Shortly before six o'clock that late-March night, the pavement across the way from the Haymarket Hotel was adorned by the presence of a shabby but impressive figure clad in flowing robes and sandals, hairy and bearded as a desert patriarch, and carrying a crudely lettered sign reading: "Repent For the End Is Near." The prophet of doom cast frequent glances both at all who traversed that particular section of sidewalk and at the window of a certain third-floor room in the hotel.

At six precisely, a young man in a flamboyant suit

and tweed cap stopped for a moment nearby, looking across the street. The curtain in the third-floor window moved, and a woman who now stood framed in it nodded her head once, slowly. The young man immediately stepped out into the street and halted a passing cab, climbed into it, and was driven off.

The robed man, his beard flying, raced into the traffic, waving his sign frantically, and calling, "Cab! Cab!"

Some twenty minutes later, the young man's cab deposited him at the same dank waterfront area that the theater doorman had visted two days earlier. He slipped into the alleyway, and thus missed seeing a second cab disgorge the old religious fanatic who had briefly shared the pavement opposite the Haymarket Hotel with him.

The bewhiskered man, still carrying his sign, looked about him with interest.

"Of course," he murmured. "Moriarty's attraction to rat-infested buildings at the water's edge. Some vestige of his ancestry, perhaps."

A few minutes later, the sound of a creaking door alerted him, and he stepped back into a shadowed doorway. As the young man emerged from the alley once more, he was suddenly confronted by the bearded man, whose ascetic appearance was marred by the very businesslike revolver he had produced from his robes and had trained on the young man's head.

"Charles Nickers, I presume," said the prophet. "My name is Sherlock Holmes. I dare say you've heard of me."

"Gor blimey!" was all that Nickers could say.

"Yes, I often wonder why He hasn't chosen to do just that on many an occasion . . . Now then, my man, unless you wish to go the way of your brother, Bill, tell me who is in that building!"

"The . . . the Professor . . ."

"And how many others? Speak up smartly, or you'll swing for it!"

Holmes did not see an upstairs window in the

moldering building slide partly open, or a pallid face crowned with wispy white hair stare out at the scene below, and then become distorted with rage. Professor Moriarty watched his bizarrely clad enemy march his underling off to the next street in search of a policeman, and, quivering with fury, sank back into the chair behind his desk. A pawn had been taken, and soon most of his pieces might be swept from the board—but Sherlock Holmes was a long way from placing James Moriarty in check!

A block away, Holmes was handing over his prisoner to an astonished New York policeman.

"Here's my card, constable. Take this man in charge and get word at once to Inspector Lafferty that the building at the far end of this alley is to be surrounded and its occupants arrested. Tell him that I'll provide him with full details directly."

The policeman had trouble enough taking in this unusual message, but the name on the card, contrasted with the outlandish figure before him, was even harder to credit.

He looked from the pasteboard to the prophet, and said, faintly, "You *are?*"

A quarter of an hour after this encounter, Sherlock Holmes, still robed, sandalled and bearded and carrying his sign, descended from a cab in front of number 4, Gramercy Park West, and made for the steps leading to the house. Hesitating, he crossed the street, and strode up to the still-present watcher in the checked suit, who eyed him curiously, then ducked as the sign was thrust in front of his eyes.

"I strongly suggest you take these words to heart, my man!" said Holmes in an eerie, quavering voice.

He then re-crossed the street and entered the house, leaving Moriarty's spy wondering what sort of crazy crew was gathering at the Adler woman's lodgings.

Inside, Sherlock Holmes quickly penned a note outlining his discoveries and emphasizing the need for immediate action on Moriarty and his henchmen, sealed it, and passed it to the waiting butler.

"There you are, Heller. To Inspector Lafferty as quickly as possible!"

"Yes, sir." As the man hurried out with the note, Holmes began to remove his beard and wig. To Irene Adler, standing close to him with young Scott, he said, "Within the half-hour, Moriarty and his entire American organization will be in custody. Irene, your fears are at an end."

He looked down at Scott and put his hands on the boy's shoulders.

"Well, well, young man, you've had more than an adventure—much more! You've aided in the capture of the world's most notorious criminal, and you've been instrumental in preventing a devastating world war."

"Well, I wish I'd known all that, sir," said the boy. "I wouldn't have slept through so much of it!"

"Well said!" Holmes turned to Irene Adler. "Bright lad. Well, I must be off now. Good-bye, Scott."

"Good-bye, Mr. Holmes."

"Must you go?" said Irene Adler.

Holmes, nearly through the archway, indicated his costume.

"Yes. These must go back to the costumer, and I'm anxious to learn of Inspector Lafferty's success."

Irene Adler nodded, and followed him through the arch, walking beside him down the stairs. Halfway in the descent, he paused and looked throughtfully at her.

"You've not changed, really," said he, "since that week in Montenegro . . . when was it, 'ninety-one?"

"Not changed in ten years? Sherlock, how gallant of you. But come, now—ten years?"

"I notice nothing."

There was an undertone of laughter in her voice. "What? Sherlock Holmes notices nothing?"

"Why, am *I* so different, then?"

"No. Far from it. That was my first thought when

you burst in here: My heavens, it's as though it were yesterday!"

"Well, then?" He studied the woman for a moment, seemed about to continue down the stairs, and then glanced back toward the drawing-room and the now unseen Scott. "I hadn't known . . . after that first misadventure from which I managed to extricate you . . . that you'd married again."

She held his gaze steadily.

"I have never remarried, Sherlock."

"I see . . . You were appearing in—*Rigoletto,* wasn't it?"

Irene Adler nodded. "And you were on a walking tour."

"Yes, I remember thinking to myself, what an unlikely place to come across you: Montenegro. You were always so attracted to . . . the bright lights of the Metropolis."

"I remember thinking the same of you. What an unlikely place to come upon someone who was never at home outside of London."

Sherlock Holmes said, very softly, "Never . . . until *then,* perhaps."

Their gazes locked silently for another moment. Then Holmes reached inside his robes, fetched out his watch, and checked the time.

"Almost eight," said he. "If things have gone well, and they cannot fail to have done, I'll get word to you. Perhaps the two of us could—the *three* of us could—take supper together." He looked at her with the hint of a grin. "And I don't mean Watson."

Irene Adler held out her hand as she spoke. "I'll wait for your message."

Holmes took her fingers very gently, his face grave, as if studying and memorizing the faint, enigmatic smile she now gave him.

It was all very well for Holmes to make a point of returning his prophet's regalia to the costumers—and I suppose it wouldn't have done for him to have gone about the streets all night in it—but the result of that errand was a truly infuriating delay while the Inspector and I waited for him outside the Hotel Algonquin, a wait made even less pleasant by the doorman's evident mortification at the sight of Lafferty's police buggy parked at the curb.

When Holmes did finally appear, past nine, and looking a great deal jauntier than I recalled seeing him for some time, I am afraid that I was less than friendly in my greeting. "Holmes! Where have you been? We've been waiting God knows how long!"

"What is it?" he replied, clearly startled by my vehemence. He glanced with concern at Lafferty. "Didn't you get my message, Inspector?"

"I did, Mr. Holmes, and the Nickers fellow revealed the name of McGraw's man who's been co-operating with Moriarty. He's been arrested, the warehouse has been seized, and fifteen of Moriarty's henchmen are in jail right now."

"But not Moriarty!" I cried.

"What! Is that true?"

"I'm afraid so," said the Inspector. "He abandoned his men and slipped through our net."

Holmes' face went stiff with sudden fear.

"We must get to Irene's house on the instant! Scott Adler is in the most extreme peril!"

Lafferty did not question his judgment, but pointed to the buggy and cried out, "The wagon! Quick!"

The three of us jumped aboard, and in a moment were clattering down the street. It was but a few moments—peril-filled ones, they seemed to me, as we dashed through the evening traffic and careered around corners so quickly that the buggy at times canted over on two wheels—until we drew up at Irene Adler's house and Holmes dashed up the steps, ringing the bell and calling for her and Scott.

"But—they're not here, Mr. Holmes," answered the perplexed Heller, looking past him at the Inspector and myself, and the buggy with its lathered horse panting in the traces.

"Not here? Where did they go?"

Holmes made his way into the foyer, and Lafferty and I followed.

"Why—to meet you, sir. You sent them this telegram."

The butler picked up a buff-colored sheet of paper from the foyer table.

"Give me that!" cried Holmes, and hastily read it. " 'Meet me at the fountain in Stuyvesant Square within the hour. Sherlock.' " He crumpled the telegram in his fist. "I've sent them directly into his hands! Heller—how long ago did they leave?"

"Within the half-hour, sir."

Sherlock Holmes turned to us, his eyes ablaze.

"Quick, The game's afoot, and we've not a moment to lose!"

Chapter Fourteen

Holmes, Lafferty, and I scurried down the steps to the buggy and leaped aboard it.

The Inspector yelled to the driver, "Stuyvesant Square! Emergency!"

We were bounced about on the seat as the wagon got off to a racing start. Far faster than before, we scorched through the streets, very nearly overturning at some corners, it seemed to me, and more than once scraping a lamppost.

In a few moments, Lafferty glanced out the window and said, "This is it! Now, where—?"

I looked out into the park-like square, and saw, near its central fountain, the figure of a lone woman.

"There! That's Miss Adler. But where's the boy?"

At the Inspector's direction, the driver sent the police wagon driving straight along the footpath to where Irene Adler stood. Holmes fairly tumbled out of it and ran over to her.

"Sherlock! Sherlock, they have him! They have him again! Just now!"

I caught a glimpse of a closed carriage at the moment leaving the square, the lamplight revealing a familiar checked pattern on the driver's coat, and pointed at it.

"Holmes! There, just turning the corner! The chap driving that cab!"

"Yes!" cried Irene Adler. "They're the ones!"

"Moriarty!" said Holmes. "Inspector! That cab! We must overtake it! Irene, Watson, come!"

He and I pulled her along and into the buggy, while

Lafferty called out to his driver, "That cab heading south! Catch up with it!"

Once again the police vehicle seemed to fly along the streets; but this time there was a quarry in sight, a quarry which, though we could not gain on it, did not seem able to draw away from us.

In a few broken sentences, Irene Adler told us how she had taken the telegram as a genuine one, thinking that Holmes, to celebrate Moriarty's downfall, meant to meet them at the indicated spot to take them to the late supper he had spoken of. She and her son had, indeed, thought that the carriage which approached them held Holmes himself, until the boy had been snatched from her and thrust into the cab by the man in the bright suit, and she herself immobilized by a pistol clapped to her head.

"Thank God you came when you did!" she gasped. "Even seconds later, and they would have been out of sight and gone forever!"

"Seconds earlier, and we should have forestalled them!" said Holmes savagely. "Don't worry, Irene— we'll get your lad out of this!"

I hoped his voice did not ring as hollowly to her as it did to me.

Then, as the chase progressed, Holmes suddenly glanced sharply out the window.

"Inspector, isn't this—?" he began.

"By heaven, it is," said Lafferty. "We're heading straight for the scoundrel's headquarters!"

The carriage containing Scott Adler and the white-faced man who menaced him with a pistol, and driven by the man in the checked suit, jolted to a halt at the derelict warehouse.

"They're hot on our heels, Professor!" the driver called.

"Step lively, boy!" Moriarty ordered Scott. "Through that door and up the stairs! March!"

The driver pulled the door closed behind them.

In the Professor's study, Moriarty snapped orders to his remaining henchman.

"You know what to do! Ready the launch!"

He grasped a long lever at the side of his desk and pulled it. A section of the bookshelves along one wall slid open, revealing a moldy, brick-lined passage. The man in the checked suit entered it and was lost to sight.

"We'll follow, once I've completed one final bit of business," said Moriarty. He flung an arm around the boy's neck and dragged him behind the desk, then raised his pistol and barked, "Don't move, boy! It'll be the finish of you if you do!"

His weapon trained on the door, he waited . . .

As the police buggy dashed up, to halt beside the now-empty carriage that had brought Scott Adler and his captors to this dreadful place, the four of us jumped from it.

Lafferty ordered his driver, "Round up a squad as fast as you can!" The buggy turned and clattered off once more. "Shall we burst in and seize them?" he asked Holmes.

"No! I must go in alone. Who knows what harm he might do Scott if cornered—and I'm sure the premises blaze with hidden pitfalls. When you see the lad come out that door—unharmed—*then* you may come in after me."

He walked toward the warehouse door, then halted briefly and turned as Irene Adler moaned hopelessly, "Oh, Scott, Scott . . . !"

"You shall not long be parted."

Holmes said the phrase as solemnly as a man taking an oath.

He moved cautiously but certainly up the steps. Light leaked around a door at the edge of the landing, and he knew that here was where the final confrontation must be. Once at the door, he did not hesitate, but pushed it open.

Professor James Moriarty, a gun trained squarely at Holmes' chest, and grasping Scott Adler about the throat, sat crouched behind his desk.

"Mr. Sherlock Holmes!" said he in venomous, husky tones. "I thought it might be you."

"I've no doubt of that at all." Holmes looked about the room, and a touch of grim amusement passed across his face. "Well, well! A little touch of London far from home, I see! You must really feel at home in that chamber of horrors to want to duplicate it wherever you go." He took one step nearer the desk. "You may release the lad now, Professor. *I'm* the one you want, and here I stand. Let the boy return to his mother."

Moriarty sneered.

"Dare you cross the room to fetch him?"

Sherlock Holmes took another step. With the speed of a striking cobra, Moriarty let his pistol fall to the desk, gave a sudden tug at one of the levers protruding from its edge, and snatched the weapon up again. Holmes leaped to one side just in time to avoid the smashing plunge of the heavy chandelier to the floor.

"Wrong, Mr. Holmes!" cried Moriarty in shrilly triumphant tones. "I've *got* what I want—the boy!" He indicated the open passageway with the pistol, then returned it to its bead on Holmes. "D'you see that passage? It leads to the river, where a steam launch waits! The boy comes with me, and you'll never see him again, neither you nor his mother! *That's* the revenge I'll have of you, Mr. Holmes! You'll neither of you ever see this precious boy again!"

Holmes' leap had brought him next to the mantelpiece, on which, he noticed, stood a vase identical to the one he had smashed in the Professor's London quarters. He reached for it—and flung it squarely at the hand which held the gun. It shattered, and Moriarty gave a howl as the weapon spun to the floor. In making a grab for it, he momentarily released his grip on Scott.

"Scott! Run!" Holmes cried, leaping at Moriarty.

"Back down those stairs to your mother! Quick, lad—show me your heels!"

As the boy disappeared, Holmes and Moriarty grappled in what each meant to be their final struggle. The Professor snatched the gun from the floor as Holmes closed with him, forced his arm upwards, and the pistol fired harmlessly into the ceiling. Holmes was able to wrench it away from him, and flung it aside; then Moriarty broke free, grabbed an umbrella from a stand and brought it down in a vicious arc aimed at his opponent's head. Holmes parried the blow and struck the umbrella from his adversary's hands.

The struggle had taken them almost to the fireplace, against which the Professor now violently shoved Holmes. Then Moriarty darted back to his desk to pull another lever, which sent a knife flashing across the room to within a fraction of an inch of the detective's head. Holmes grabbed up a fire iron and advanced on Moriarty, but was obliged to leap backwards to avoid the impact of a heavy suit of standing armor which the Professor attempted to tip over onto him.

With another bound to his desk, Moriarty gave a final tug to a lever, and the section of flooring immediately behind Holmes—in fact, partly under his heels—dropped away, leaving him teetering precariously. Moriarty gave a savage roar of triumph and rushed for him. Together they grappled, and swayed on the edge of the open trap door, as they had on that May day ten years before, on the brink of the Reichenbach Falls.

Outside the warehouse, the police driver had just returned with a half-dozen reinforcing constables, when we heard a shot, and then saw Scott Adler suddenly appear in the doorway. Irene Adler cried out and ran to him, dropping to her knees and enveloping him in her arms.

"I'm going in there, Inspector," said I firmly.

I strode for the door, somewhat relieved to see that Lafferty and his men were hard on my heels. We took the stairs at a run, and burst into the room at their top—to see Holmes and Professor Moriarty locked in a precarious struggle over a gaping trap door.

Lafferty drew a pistol and shouted, "Professor Moriarty—throw up your hands!"

Unhappily, this diversion startled Holmes more than it did the Professor, who seized the opportunity to force him over the edge of the trap. With a yell, Holmes dropped from sight—but then I saw his fingers, still grasping the edge of the flooring.

"Holmes! Great heavens!" I cried, and flung myself down, managing to get a grip on my friend's wrists. "Here! Give us a hand, some of you!" I called over my shoulder, and Lafferty and his driver each got a hold on one of my legs and hauled backwards, perforce drawing Holmes out of the open trap.

Many hands now reached out to help us both to our feet, but abruptly Sherlock Holmes whirled and pointed to an open passageway in the wall.

"Quick! He's getting away!"

We turned and saw Moriarty slinking down the passage. Holmes leaped to follow, but Moriarty, with a high-pitched cackle, threw a lever protruding from the wall, and a closely knit mesh of steel wire crashed down, blocking our entrance.

"Good night, Mr. Sherlock Holmes!" the Professor called out.

Inspector Lafferty gave an inarticulate roar and emptied his revolver at Moriarty—who could, after the volley, be seen standing unhurt behind the mesh curtain. His taunting voice came through it clearly.

"Let the victory be yours this time, Mr. Holmes. But there will be other battles and other battlefields, and victory's so temporary a thing, is it not? Good night, Mr. Sherlock Holmes!"

Professor James Moriarty seemed to shimmer in the gloom of the passage, and then was gone.

"Where in the world can it lead to, Holmes?" said I.

"To the river, Watson—where a steam launch waits." My friend's voice was quiet, and weary.

Inspector Lafferty was fuming.

"I'll have a police vessel in his wake within the hour!" he exclaimed.

Sherlock Holmes shook his head.

"Within half that time, he'll undoubtedly be beyond the limits of your jurisdiction. No. The final encounter between the Professor and myself is yet to come. In any event, I am assured of the boy's safety." He faced me and set one hand on my shoulder. "Watson, I am once again deeply in your debt. That tide would soon have carried me to my certain end."

I was pleased almost to bursting at his words, but could find nothing better to say than a mumbled, "My pleasure, Holmes. Don't mention it."

He turned back to the Inspector.

"Our quarry may have eluded us, but his evil scheme has been thwarted. At what time is the transfer of the gold to take place?"

Lafferty scanned Holmes' face anxiously.

"At eleven tomorrow morning!" he answered.

Holmes smiled at him.

"Then let us all be there to witness it. I assure you that I am not jesting, and that you shall not be disappointed."

Chapter Fifteen

The lift that connected the ground floor of the Bouwerie National Bank with the gold vaults below it was thronged to capacity the next morning, with Holmes and myself, Inspector Lafferty, Mortimer McGraw, three Exchange employees, and one representive each of the German and Italian banks who were concerned in the approaching transaction.

Although both Lafferty and McGraw were clearly close to panic with anxiety, Holmes was chatting amiably with the latter.

". . . Yes, Lord Brackish, Managing Director of the Bank of England. He was to be murdered mysteriously, and his death was to cause panic in the world's financial circles. *This* theft was to be the culmination of a grand scheme. I was able to foil the murder of Brackish, and I am now able to forestall the theft of the gold."

"Mr. Holmes," said McGraw tensely, "I certainly hope your confidence is not over-expressed."

The lift shuddered to a halt.

"You may test its validity at your convenience, Mr. McGraw, for we seem to have arrived. Be so good as to unlock the door."

McGraw closed his eyes for a brief moment, as if in prayer, then opened them and, with less than accustomed expertness, worked the combination lock and pushed the heavy steel door open.

The Italian and German representatives, who were familiar with the vaults, saw nothing out of the ordinary. As expected, there were the neat rows of cells, each door tightly shut, the dull glint of gold visible through the bars on each, the whole culminating in a very solid and unbreached rear wall.

The effect on Lafferty, McGraw, and the three Exchange employees was considerably different. Though, in varying ways, they all expressed stupefied surprise, it was quickly controlled, lest it raise questions in the minds of the foreign bankers which they would find it awkward to answer.

Holmes, clearly savoring all this, leaned down and whispered in my ear, "Last night, round about midnight, I slipped into the false chamber and removed the bars that kept the lift from descending to its rightful place. Good job no one saw me, eh? Think what the papers would have made of that!"

He turned to the still-speechless Lafferty and McGraw.

"Well, gentlemen," he half whispered. "All present and accounted for? No delusion, no sleight-of-hand, no mirage? If you're satisfied the gold has been returned, Dr. Watson and I have a busy day ahead of us, as it will be our last one before returning home."

"Surely," said McGraw, confusion and wonderment still written on his face, "you'll do me the honor of dining with me?"

"I fear not, Mr. McGraw. This evening, we—and a young lad of our acquaintance—have tickets for *The Second Mrs. Tanqueray.*"

He made as if to re-enter the lift, and Inspector Lafferty stepped in front of him, nearly frantic with curiosity.

"Mr. Holmes! Aren't you going to explain how you did this?"

The detective gave him a gentle smile.

"No. But I expect one day Dr. Watson will."

After the curtain had fallen on that night's performance of *The Second Mrs. Tanqueray,* its leading lady sat at her dressing table, removing her stage makeup. The light-framed mirror showed her a tall man in evening dress standing behind her.

To the image, she said, "Must you really leave at once?"

"I'm afraid so. So many things in England demand my attention just now."

"All of which you abandoned to race to my rescue. Sherlock, now that I'm rescued, can't you stay a while to enjoy your success?"

Holmes shook his head.

"I wish I could. But the *Etruria* sails at midnight, and Watson will soon be along in a carriage to fetch me."

"What are you running from, Sherlock?"

"Running from? Inactivity, I suppose . . . boredom . . ."

The last of the make-up creamed away, she turned to face him directly.

"Are you certain it's not . . . fear?"

"Fear? Of what?"

"Perhaps the unknown."

Holmes gave a mirthless chuckle.

"My dear Irene, it's the *known* I fear! I *seek* the unknown. An unknown mystery, an unknown peril. I *long* for the unknown!"

"And for nothing else?" She looked intently up into his eyes. "Sherlock—is there nothing you would like to ask me?"

The man was silent for a moment, then spoke hesitantly.

"Yes . . . but I cannot."

"Why?"

"Because of the answer I might receive."

"I see." Irene Adler turned back to her mirror, her face a little more set in its lines than a moment before. "Well, then, if you cannot ask it, I cannot answer it."

Holmes regarded her concentratedly.

"And if I *were* to ask it?" he asked quietly.

Her gaze came to him through the mirror.

"And if the answer were the wrong one?" She smiled ruefully. "You see, perhaps I too am in fear of . . . the known." She inspected her face in the mirror, and appeared to find a trace of cosmetic missed before. "Shall we meet again, do you think?"

"I should be happy to believe so. Shall I continue to receive theater tickets?"

"So long as I continue to perform."

"And perhaps with a word or two included . . . about the boy?"

"I'd be most happy to."

"Likable little chap, you know," Holmes said carelessly.

"Do you think so?" Irene Adler's brows arched slightly in wry amusement.

"What are his interests, mainly?"

She was silent a moment, and then said evenly, "He seems to have a fondness for music . . . and for solving problems."

"I see. Would you, perhaps, have an extra . . . picture of the lad?"

She turned once more to face Holmes. Then she opened the locket that hung at her throat, extracted a small oval of stiff paper, and handed it to him.

"Take this one."

Holmes studied the miniature photograph. "But this must be your favorite."

"It is."

"Thank you. I shall treasure it." Holmes pulled out his watch, opened the cover, and placed the picture inside. Then he looked at the face of the watch. Irene Adler followed his glance, then nodded.

"I know," she said.

She rose and held out both hands to him. Sherlock Holmes grasped them, and stood silently for a moment. Their gazes met fully.

"Irene . . . ?"

"Yes?"

Holmes took a deep breath, then let it go. "Good-bye."

"Good-bye, Sherlock."

Rattling along in the four-wheeler that should set us down at the *Etruria*'s pier in a few moments, I felt both exhilarated and let-down. It had certainly been an eventful few days in New York, and I had found much to admire in the city. But, after all, it wasn't London! And, while new experiences are all very well, I find that the old ones, and the old, familiar ways of doing things, suit best in the end.

I noticed Holmes consulting his watch, and commented on it.

"Yes, by Jove," I said, "two hours and we're out to sea, a few more days and we're back in Baker Street—back where you can drink a proper cup of tea, even travel by Underground if it suits your purpose. This is said to be a splendid city, Holmes, and I dare say it is in many ways. But when it comes down to it, does it have anything worthwhile that we don't have in London?"

Holmes looked down again at his watch, and ran the tip of his forefinger gently over something in the case.

"Perhaps not, Watson. Perhaps not."

Indefatigable. Intelligent. Immortal.

by Sir Arthur Conan Doyle

Available at your bookstore or use this coupon.

___ **THE SEVEN-PER-CENT SOLUTION**, Nicholas Meyer 25588 1.95
Sherlock Holmes meets Sigmund Freud in this, his most incredible case. At stake are Holmes's mental health and the political future of the Balkans. This #1 bestseller is "a pure delight!"—Chicago News

___ **A STUDY IN SCARLET**, Introduction by Ed McBain 24714 1.25
Who killed the two American travellers . . . and how does Holmes, in London, unravel a mystery that began in the desert wastes of Utah, spread to the capital cities of Europe and came to a fatal climax in England?

___ **THE SIGN OF THE FOUR**, Introduction by P. G. Wodehouse 24715 1.25
On the trail of a mysterious treasure, Holmes and Watson discover the murder of the treasure's custodian. Murder in a room bolted from the inside. And the treasure itself had vanished!

___ **ADVENTURES OF SHERLOCK HOLMES**,
Introduction by Ellery Queen 24716 1.25
A collection of classic mystery thrillers, including A Scandal in Bohemia, The Red-Headed League, The Five Orange Pips, and nine other unforgettable Holmes adventures!

___ **MEMOIRS OF SHERLOCK HOLMES**, Introduction by Joe Gores 24717 1.25
More classic mystery adventures, including The Musgrave Ritual, Silver Blaze, The Crooked Man and eight more of the best Holmes thrillers!

___ **THE HOUND OF THE BASKERVILLES**,
Introduction by Don Pendleton 24718 1.25
Holmes and Watson investigate the strange case of Henry Baskerville. The new lord of the Manor of Baskerville had been warned not to claim his inheritance . . . on pain of death from the ancient curse that killed his ancestors.

___ **THE RETURN OF SHERLOCK HOLMES**, Introduction by Nicholas Meyer, author of The Seven-Per-Cent Solution 24719 1.25
Thirteen masterpieces of Holmesian detection, including The Adventure of The Empty House, The Dancing Men, and The Six Napoleons.

BB Ballantine Mail Sales
Dept. LE, 201 E. 50th Street
New York, New York 10022

Please send me the books I have checked above. I am enclosing
$............ .... (please add 50¢ to cover postage and handling).
Send check or money order—no cash or C.O.D.'s please.

Name_____

Address_____

City_____ State_____ Zip_____

Please allow 4 weeks for delivery.

L-49-76

FICTION *for all seasons... for people of all ages.*

Available at your bookstore or use this coupon.

___ **THE LAST UNICORN, Peter Beagle** 25484 1.75
A unicorn's quest for her lost fellows, this is a fantasy classic. ALA, Notable Book of the Year. "Beagle is a true magician with words...."
—Granville Hicks, SATURDAY REVIEW

___ **FAHRENHEIT 451, Ray Bradbury** 25027 1.50
A modern classic depicting a future in which censorship has gone wild. "Frightening in its implications ... fascinating."—NEW YORK TIMES

___ **ECHOES OF A SUMMER, William Johnston** 25633 1.50
The moving, courageous story of a girl on the brink of womanhood and on the brink of death who finds the real meaning of love and life itself.

___ **THE SON OF SOMEONE FAMOUS, M. E. Kerr** 25631 1.25
A wacky but tender novel of two self-proclaimed social misfits. "M. E. Kerr is a brilliant writer with an ear for the minute agonies and hilarities of adolescents...."—NEW YORK TIMES

___ **YOUNG FRANKENSTEIN, Gilbert Pearlman** 24268 1.50
Based on the screenplay by Gene Wilder and Mel Brooks, this is the terrifyingly hilarious story of Dr. Frankenstein's grandson—America's leading brain surgeon—who tries to create a death-defying creature.

___ **THE HOBBIT, J. R. R. Tolkien** 25342 1.95
The delightful tale of the imperishable world of fantasy called Middle-Earth, and those charming, indomitable creatures—the hobbits.

___ **SARAH T.—PORTRAIT OF A TEEN-AGE ALCOHOLIC, Robin S. Wagner** 25477 1.25
A novelization of the highly-successful T.V. movie about a 15-year-old girl who becomes an alcoholic when she is unable to cope with her parents' divorce and their insensitivity towards her.

BB Ballantine Mail Sales
Dept. LE, 201 E. 50th Street
New York, New York 10022

Please send me the books I have checked above. I am enclosing $....................... (please add 50¢ to cover postage and handling). Send check or money order—no cash or C.O.D.'s please.

Name_____

Address_____

City_____ State_____ Zip_____

Please allow 4 weeks for delivery.

L-40-76